I0542315

Dominion

THE ULTIMATUM

KATY SWANN

The Ultimatum
ISBN # 978-1-78430-382-2
©Copyright Katy Swann 2014
Cover Art by Posh Gosh ©Copyright December 2014
Interior text design by Claire Siemaszkiewicz
Totally Bound Publishing

Published in 2014 by Totally Bound Publishing, Newland House, The Point, Weaver Road, Lincoln, LN6 3QN, United Kingdom.

Totally Bound Publishing is a subsidiary of Totally Entwined Group Limited.

THE ULTIMATUM

Dedication

Thank you to everybody who has supported me since I started to pursue my dream of writing. From my wonderful family, dear friends, fellow authors and the lovely readers who have given me such positive and encouraging feedback. I do truly appreciate it.

Prologue

Frankie Hamilton glared at her husband in irritation. What the hell did he want to drag her off to a 'romantic' weekend for? She'd been planning on catching up with some seriously overdue paperwork, not wasting time at some overpriced fancy hotel.

"Well?" Jake's dark blue eyes flashed with equal amounts of determination and hope.

She looked at him, giving him her best 'don't be so ridiculous' look and spoke in a calm, low voice, "Jake, sweetie, it's a bit short notice. I know it's bank holiday weekend, but I've still got work to do."

"No you don't. I checked with Jess."

Frankie scowled at him, her irritation turning to anger. *How dare he call my secretary behind my back?* She made a mental note to have a serious word with Jess about discretion on Tuesday morning but there was a more immediate problem that needed to be dealt with.

"Look, it's Friday evening, so let's just enjoy it and have an early night instead, huh?" She slunk sexily up to him and gave him a seductive kiss on the lips. Usually a quick fuck was enough to shut him up and so she confidently fluttered her eyelashes, sure in the knowledge that her feminine charm would work its magic.

As she rubbed her toned body against Jake's hard torso, she moved her hand down to his crotch. Maybe she could get away with a quick hand job? The sooner she could get back to finishing her report, the better.

But, as she searched for his bulge, he pushed her roughly away. A quick glance down told her there was no bulge. Was she losing her touch?

"You have a choice, Frankie — you either come with me this weekend, or I leave. Permanently. Do you understand?" His voice was icy as he spoke.

Even as a shiver of unease ran through her body at his words, she stamped on the impact they'd had. He wouldn't leave her. *No way! Would he?*

But before she'd had a chance to formulate a reply, he grabbed a fistful of her hair and tugged, not too hard, but hard enough to make her freeze. She shuddered when she felt his warm breath on her ear as he spoke again.

"I said, do you understand?" The words came out in a low growl, and her knees weakened slightly as memories of the same words spoken in the same tone crashed back with startling clarity.

She's on her knees, naked and trembling with lust as Jake holds her head firmly in place.

"Do you understand?" he growls, his eyes flashing dangerously.

"Yes, Master," she gasps as she melts under his strong, dominant glare. The only thing that matters is pleasing him and that means obeying him without question. Oh yes...

She quickly shook the memory off and pulled away from his grip. If he thought she was going to submit again, he had another thing coming.

"Jake, for God's sake, stop playing games." Although her voice sounded strong and confident, a little seed of uncertainty had planted itself in the back of her head. It had been a long time since she'd seen Jake so determined about something and she knew him well enough to know that he wouldn't issue such an ultimatum if he didn't mean it. Would he really leave her?

They'd been through so much in their six years of marriage. They'd been happy at first, balancing their blossoming careers with their passionate sex life. They hadn't been able to get enough of each other, both in and out of the bedroom. And the day he'd confessed his dark desires things had gotten even better.

"I'm a Dom, Frankie," he says, running a hand through her hair.

She giggles. "A what?"

There's a fire in his eyes as he almost growls his reply, "I like to take control in the bedroom. I want to dominate you, put you over my knee and spank your bare bottom until it's glowing red."

"Oh."

He pulls her into his arms and holds onto her tightly. Then he whispers, "I want to tie you to the bed so you're helpless and completely at my mercy. Then I'll fuck you until you scream from coming so hard."

"Mmm, yes please." There's a hot throbbing ache in her pussy as she imagines herself restrained and under his control.

"Pardon?"

The look of surprise on his face is hilarious.

"I'm serious, Jake. I want you to spank me. I want you to tie me up. Damn it, I want you to dominate me."

She'd meant it and she'd loved it when he had done just that. That had been the beginning of a beautiful new dynamic in their lives. The more she'd surrendered her control to Jake the happier she'd been until, two years later, he'd moved things to a new level. She blinked at the memory then raised her hand and touched the base of her neck, the same place where her permanent collar would have symbolized their new status.

"Will you be my slave, Frankie? Twenty-four-seven?

She's tied to a discreet hook hidden behind the bedroom door. If she had the freedom of movement she'd throw herself into his arms but, as she's unable to do that, she nods through tears of happiness.

"Oh yes, Sir. I'd love that more than anything in the world."

But the formal collaring ceremony they had planned for later that year had never happened, and suddenly, tragically, everything had changed.

How had talks of a possible total power exchange ended in an, almost, reversal of roles? She was the boss now — she paid most of the bills and she instigated sex — although admittedly usually just as a means to getting her own way.

Jake's cool voice spoke again and she reluctantly turned her attention back to him.

"No games, Frankie. We leave for Kent tomorrow afternoon and if you're not with me, the next time you'll hear from me will be through my lawyer. I'm going out now. Call me when you've decided what's more important." His eyes bored into hers, sending a clear subliminal message. He was serious.

She stood rooted to the spot in shock for quite a few minutes after he'd stormed out of the room. Suddenly the front door slammed and she jumped, startled. Then she slowly sank onto the bed and, for the first time in years, tears filled her eyes as she acknowledged the very real crisis her marriage was in.

Maybe she should let him go without her? After all, if there really was no future for them, they might as well end it now and save any more heartache. But the thought of losing him forever sent a surprising surge of panic through her. Did she really want him to go? Did he still love her? More to the point, did she still love him?

Subconsciously, she twisted the gold band on her finger. The day Jake had slipped it on had been the happiest of her life. She had meant it when she'd told him that she would always love him, no matter what, and she'd known his undying words of love were just as heartfelt and genuine as her own.

She owed it to him to go along this weekend to see if they could save their failing marriage. But even as she thought it, her mind drifted back to the report waiting on her laptop to be finished. *Damn! What should I do?*

She remained seated on the bed for a very long time, her dilemma taunting her as she struggled to accept that something had to change. Then, quite suddenly, she knew what she had to do. With her decision made, she rose, reached for her phone then scrolled down to Jake's number.

* * * *

Jake didn't know where he was going, he just knew he needed to get out of the house. Away from Frankie. As he headed toward the High Street, he realized he was walking in the direction of the pub, but on reflection that probably wasn't such a good idea as it would be too tempting to drown his sorrows in whiskey. No, he needed a clear head because he wasn't going to back down this time.

A family in front of him were being dragged toward a small park by a large German Shepherd, so without thinking too deeply about it he followed them through the gates. At least it was somewhere quiet where he could gather his thoughts while he waited for Frankie's call. He checked his phone was switched on and found a bench near the playground.

He and Frankie had gone for many walks through this park in the early days of their marriage.

They're strolling, hand in hand, smiling at the mothers pushing their babies in their state-of-the-art prams.

Frankie giggles as they pass a particularly fancy one with a chrome frame and the well-known brand clearly printed for all to see. "It seems that, like four-by-four cars, there's an unspoken rule of keeping up with the other parents by aspiring to have the biggest and most technically advanced buggy," she whispers.

He laughs. "Yeah, surely the kid doesn't give two hoots what buggy they're in."

They walk past another parent with a three-wheeled contraption that looks like something from another planet, and they both smile knowingly.

Now, though, he didn't smile. He looked away from the parents, the children and the buggies, not wanting to be reminded of those times. A familiar knot tightened in his throat and he turned his thoughts back to Frankie and the ultimatum he had just given her. Had he done the right thing? He was only too well aware that it could backfire badly — she might tell him to get lost.

His attention was drawn to a man a few meters down the path, teaching his son to ride a bike. He was laughing as the boy begged him not to let go, unaware that he already had. Jake would do the same thing with his own child one day if…

He shook his head as if to shake away the thought. No, he mustn't start thinking about that now. He looked at the display on his phone, just in case he'd somehow missed the loud, jangling ring tone, but it remained blank. No missed calls.

He loved Frankie so much and didn't want to lose her, but he knew that if he let things carry on the way they were, they would grow even further apart and he couldn't bear that. That damned business of hers had driven a wedge between them. He'd been supportive at first, knowing she'd needed an outlet for her grief, but she had thrown herself so heavily into the business that she no longer had time for him.

Losing their baby when Frankie had been eleven weeks pregnant had knocked their world off kilter. The grief was still as strong now as it had been then. Every time he saw a baby he felt as though a knife sliced through him reminding him of the pain of what they'd lost. People had told him the pain would get better but they'd been wrong. It still fucking hurt like hell.

"Shh, sweetheart," he soothes and tightens his hold around her. "The doctors say there's no obvious reason why we can't try for another baby in the future."

"But what if it happens again?" she cries, tears rolling freely down her face.

"It won't," he tries to reassure her. But, of course, he doesn't know that. What if it does happen again? To go through something like that once is bad enough, but twice?

He shuddered at the memory. Apart from the heartbreak that had followed, Frankie had bled for nearly two weeks and had suffered unbearable cramps. It had practically destroyed her. How could they risk that again?

They should have comforted each other, but instead of the mutual support they'd both needed, they had locked themselves out of each other's hearts and sought solace in their work. Ironically, he'd written his most successful book around that time, but neither he nor Frankie had enjoyed its success when it had become an international bestseller.

She'd withdrawn even further from him, and slowly the beautiful, funny and warm woman he had fallen in love with had turned into a cold, hard-headed businesswoman.

He loved her so much, but he couldn't carry on living the way they were. It was just too painful. There was no laughter anymore, no affection. Even the sex had turned cold. In the past, she had submitted so beautifully, but now, she'd probably knock him out if he dared order her to her knees. But that was exactly what he was about to do this weekend.

He thought he'd sensed a chink in her armor earlier when he'd seen her shiver at his words. Maybe it wasn't too late? That was why he wanted her to come with him this weekend. If she chose to come, it could be a sign that she was willing to try to save their marriage. He had to know.

He felt a wry smile play on his lips as he thought about what her reaction might be when she realized he had taken her to a BDSM themed hotel. She wouldn't be impressed. She'd be even less impressed when he demanded that she submit to him one more time.

But it would have to be of her own free will. He wasn't going to force her, that wasn't his style. If he could convince her to submit to him again, it might just help to break down some of those icy barriers she had erected around her heart. She had always been so open and honest about her feelings when she had been in a submissive headspace, and that was what he was hoping for now. After that, if she didn't want to continue with a D/s relationship, he would accept and respect that, as long as their marriage was back on track.

She was a natural submissive, though. Hell, she'd even agreed to be his slave once, which was why he hoped that asking her to submit again would help her to rediscover her true sexuality.

He stared blankly at a couple of dogs sniffing each other's shit. They might as well have been dancing the tango for all he cared. His mind was so focused on Frankie and the phone call he hoped he was about to get.

It had been a stroke of luck when he'd bumped into his old friend Marco a couple of months ago. He'd been attending a midweek writing workshop at an upmarket country house hotel in Kent. It had been a two-day event so he'd stayed over, relieved to get away from Frankie's bad moods for a while.

After dinner, he had gone for a stroll through the extensive grounds. He'd been deep in thought and hadn't noticed the man approaching him until it had been too late. He had quite literally bumped into Marco. It must have been more than two years since he'd last seen him and Jake had been genuinely pleased to meet his old friend. Marco had insisted on buying him a drink and had taken him to a private corner of the bar where all the staff seemed to know Marco by name.

Jake had been rather surprised to see Marco in such a formal environment. An ex rock star and well-known player in the BDSM community, Marco definitely didn't fit in with the elegant and corporate image of the hotel. His long hair was still jet black and unkempt, and his many tribal tattoos were bold reminders of his wild past.

He'd laughed when Marco had told him that he owned the hotel, but when he'd then told him about his second business, a hopeful plan had started to form in his head. It turned out that, although Marco owned the hotel, he didn't run the business side of it during the week. He left that to an army of efficient managers. But he did run the business at weekends, when Morgan Manor became Dominion, an exclusive BDSM themed hotel.

Marco had invited him and Frankie to come and stay any time, and Jake had finally taken his old friend up on the offer. Now, all he needed was for Frankie to agree to go. Tapping his foot restlessly, he checked his phone again and, at that moment, it rang, making him jump. He stared at it blankly for a couple of seconds. It was Frankie—this was it. Taking a deep breath to steady his nerves, he tentatively pressed the green button and answered the call.

Chapter One

The long, sweeping drive leading up to the enormous house was impressive, and Frankie silently — and grudgingly — admitted to herself that Morgan Manor was stunning. The extensive grounds were laid with lush green lawns, and age-old oaks proudly lined the gravel drive.

As the car crunched closer toward the house, she stared in awe at the imposing mansion looming in front of them. She wasn't an expert, but she guessed it must be at least four or five hundred years old, maybe more, and would probably have been a significant stately home at one time. Large leaded windows, encased in thick, stone arched frames, glistened in the late afternoon sunshine and little ornate gargoyles grinned cheekily down at them from lichen-stained buttresses.

She glanced quickly across at Jake as she climbed out of the car and was slightly unnerved by the solemn expression on his face. He was normally quite easy to read but now she had no idea what was on his mind. His silence added to the subdued sounds of the countryside, with only a few birds letting her know that she hadn't lost the use of her ears.

Jake took her arm and led her toward the house. She didn't know why, but she had the distinct feeling that this house was hiding some secrets. Secrets that she'd bet Jake knew about but wasn't telling her. *What's he up to?*

They climbed the stone steps leading up to a heavy, oak door and, just as they approached the top step, the door opened and an impeccably groomed doorman stepped aside to allow them entry. "Good afternoon, Sir," he said to Jake, and bowed slightly.

Frankie scowled. How rude of him not to address her as well.

Jake nodded at the doorman as he led them across an enormous hallway toward an antique desk discreetly placed near a grand piano. The only sound came from the old creaking floorboards and the crackle of an open fire on the other side of the spacious hall. The burning wood, mixed with the smell of beeswax and furniture polish, added to the calm, but slightly austere, ambiance of the grand hall.

When they reached the desk, a tall, elegant lady emerged from behind a door and greeted them with a friendly smile.

"Jake. How nice to see you again." The lady's voice was warm as she shook Jake's hand before turning her gaze to Frankie. "And you must be Francesca."

"Frankie. *Mrs.* Hamilton," snapped Frankie. She was aware that Jake had stayed at the hotel for one of his writing workshops recently, but still, she wasn't impressed by this woman's over-familiarity. She thought this was supposed to be a classy establishment?

The lady ignored Frankie's clipped tone and handed Jake a card. "Sign this please."

As Jake checked them in, the lady turned back to Frankie. "I'm Cleo, manager of the East Wing."

Frankie frowned. "The East Wing?"

"That's where all the fun happens at weekends." She winked in an almost conspiratorial way then turned her attention back to Jake, who had finished signing the necessary paperwork.

"James will take you to your room now. Welcome drinks will be served at six o'clock in the drawing room. Please be prompt. In the meantime, feel free to make the most of our facilities." Cleo nodded at an older man dressed as an old-fashioned butler, who politely bowed and took their bags.

As soon as they were alone in their room, Frankie shrugged her coat off and looked around. The room was enormous, with a large bay window at one end and a stone fireplace at the other. A bigger than average four-poster bed dominated the room, its bedspread and cushions matching the heavy curtains framing the windows.

Frankie's eyes were immediately drawn to a very expensive-looking desk against the far wall and her mind wandered to the small laptop she'd secretly hidden in her bag before they'd left. If she could persuade Jake to disappear for a while, she might be able to finish the report she was working on.

Fixing a smile on her face she turned to Jake. "Why don't you go down for a swim while I unpack? I assume there's a pool?"

To her surprise, though, Jake shook his head and crossed his arms firmly across his chest. "I don't think so," he said in a low voice. "I thought we agreed—no work this weekend?"

"No. You decided. I didn't agree."

She turned her back on him to find her bag. *Let him sulk.* If he really was so fucking adamant that she stayed in this stuffy old place, he could at least allow her an hour or two to finish her work.

Jake suddenly grabbed her by the shoulders, swung her round to face him and pushed her hard against the door. She gasped, completely thrown off guard. He held her in place with a steely grip. Then he reached up, took her chin firmly in his free hand and forced her to look at him.

Outrage exploded deep inside her, but before she had a chance to express it, he clamped his lips down hard on hers and forced his tongue into her mouth. Her first instinct was to struggle, but as that was futile she remained completely immobile under his iron grip.

Then, to her horror, an old familiar heat ignited between her legs and she weakened as Jake continued to take what he wanted from her. The kiss was anything but gentle, and Frankie knew, with a sinking feeling, what that meant. Jake was in Dom mode and, damn, she was responding.

No, no, no. I can't — won't submit again. But she couldn't deny the dull ache in her pussy and her legs trembled slightly with the realization that she was enjoying Jake's rough treatment of her.

Suddenly, though, just as quickly as he'd grabbed her, he let go again, leaving her standing unsteady and speechless by the door, her lips swollen and her eyes filled with tears. Jake towered silently over her, his eyes burning with raw emotion.

"I said no work this weekend. I want your undivided attention — and your complete surrender."

His voice was gravelly and dangerous when he finally spoke.

That was when it dawned on her that she'd been set up. This was no ordinary hotel. He'd lured her here under the pretense of a romantic weekend, but she knew that when he demanded her surrender like that, he had anything but romance in mind.

Anger simmered deep inside her as his words echoed in her ears. "You bastard," she hissed. She pushed him roughly away from her then stormed toward a door she assumed led to the bathroom. But just as she reached out for the handle, Jake grabbed her from behind and practically threw her onto the bed. Without a word, he pinned her down with one hand while he pulled her skirt unceremoniously up over her thighs.

Frankie was so shocked, she didn't react at first. Was he going to force himself on her? He'd never done that before, even when they'd been in the most intense stage of their D/s relationship. She whimpered as he pulled her knickers down just far enough for him to gain access to her pussy, and when he parted her legs and thrust two fingers deep inside her, she cried out in dismay and lust.

He abruptly withdrew his fingers again and sat up. Without a word, he held his hand up in front of her face and she knew she'd lost the fight. His fingers were glistening with her arousal. He'd made his point. Even she couldn't deny the obvious evidence of her body's betrayal.

Jake watched Frankie's face change from defiance to shock as he held her eyes with his own. He *knew* it! Once a submissive, always a submissive, just like he would always be a Dom. But he couldn't be too complacent. He may have won round one, but there was a long way to go before Frankie would agree to the things he had planned for her this weekend.

And he needed to tell her about Marco. He knew she would instantly recognize their old friend when they went down to join the other guests later. Marco was very memorable—tough, even taller than himself, with muscles to match those of any professional rugby player. He'd heard plenty of women talk about his edgy good looks and powerful presence, so it was no surprise that Marco had submissives literally throwing themselves at his feet. Even Frankie hadn't been immune to his rough charm and had happily submitted when they had both topped her a couple of times in the past.

Frankie would realize that Marco's presence at this hotel wouldn't be coincidental. It was time to come clean. He looked at her outraged face and his heart contracted painfully. God, he loved her. He just prayed that she loved him enough to agree to his demands one more time.

"Jake…"

"Shut up, Frankie. For once in your life, just listen without judging or interrupting." He could hear the steel in his own voice and knew the effect it would be having on her right now. She never could resist the uncompromising tone he used as a Dom.

Her mouth opened then shut again, and he gave an inward sigh of relief that she would at least hear him out. Not that he was giving her much choice.

"I know your work is important to you, but there was a time when I was important to you too." He wanted to make his point without causing too much pain so he'd decided to completely avoid bringing up the trauma of the baby. It was too painful for both of them and stirring up the grief again might do more harm than good. No, he'd keep this simple.

"Frankie, we can't go on like this. We're like two strangers living under the same roof—we don't talk, laugh or even cry together anymore. I still love you though—a lot—and I want to try to see if there's any way we can save our marriage." He ignored her intake of breath and continued before she had a chance to make some sort of cutting remark.

"I've brought you here to try to rekindle the spark I believe is still there." He paused for effect and took a deep breath before speaking the words that could make or break them.

"I want you to submit to me one more time this weekend. I mean unconditionally, for the whole weekend. If, after that, you don't feel there's any chance of a reconciliation, I'll leave, if that's what you want."

"Why do you want me to submit to you? Why don't we just talk?" growled Frankie, her eyes flashing dangerously.

Jake sighed. If only it were that easy. "That's the problem. We never talk these days and I know you'll only try to fob me off with shit you think I want to hear. I think the only way for any honesty is to break down some of those barriers you've built up, and the only way I know of that can do that is for you to submit again. If, after that, we can work things out but you don't want to resume our D/s relationship, I'll accept that. But, right now, it all comes down to a sad but simple choice or we'll end up another divorce statistic."

She flinched at the word 'divorce'. He'd used it deliberately to see if there would be any reaction, and he was relieved to see there had been. He could tell she was struggling to take it all in. Her eyes were darting around the room, looking everywhere but at him, and she was twisting her wedding ring, the way she always did when she was unsure.

"What exactly is this place?" she asked, quietly. Whether she was genuinely interested or she was just buying some extra time, he couldn't tell.

"Remember Marco Alessi?"

Her eyes widened, telling him that she did remember. He wasn't an easy person to forget. Slowly, she nodded.

"Well, Marco owns this hotel. During the week it's a business and conference center, but at weekends the East Wing opens as an exclusive BDSM hotel. The theme this weekend is Vanilla Spice."

She giggled—a sound he hadn't heard in a while. "Vanilla Spice?"

He couldn't help grinning back as he nodded. "It's aimed at BDSM beginners or people who are a little rusty in the lifestyle. The emphasis will be on Dominance and submission as opposed to S & M. Nothing hardcore." It didn't pass him by that the first time they'd both smiled in a long while was when the subject of BDSM had come up.

"How long have you been planning this?" She sounded calmer now, less agitated.

"I bumped into Marco when I was here for the writing workshop and he invited us to visit." He saw a frown crease her brow and quickly added, "He doesn't know anything about our current relationship other than the fact that it's been a while since we played."

"Oh."

He straightened his shoulders, making sure he towered over her while she remained on the bed. Then he crossed his arms and gave her his sternest look, the one that used to turn her legs to jelly.

"So, Frankie. What's it to be? Submit or divorce?"

He held his breath as he waited for her reply and, when she opened her mouth to speak, it took all his strength not to gather her in his arms in the hope that it would affect her decision.

Chapter Two

Frankie stared open-mouthed at Jake, not trusting herself to speak. What should she do? She had imagined numerous scenarios, not dissimilar to this, over the last couple of years and had wondered how she'd react if she were faced with the possibility of them going their separate ways.

But now that she was faced with the reality of it, she wasn't so sure if splitting up was what she wanted. They'd gone through so much together. Surely it was worth giving it one more go? But staying together meant submitting again, at least for the weekend, and that was where her problem lay.

After she'd lost their precious baby, she had built up her business and a reputation as being a tough and formidable businesswoman. It had been her way of coping with the grief, but the more successful she'd become, the more she'd resented Jake for wanting her to submit to him. She couldn't explain it, but it was as if she felt that, by allowing her submissive side to come out, she would lose the tough business reputation she had worked so hard for. And, as a result, lose the respect of her colleagues and employees.

"For God's sake, Frankie," snaps Jake. "No one is going to know what goes on inside our bedroom. People would never know."

"I'd know. And it's not just about what people think, I'm just not into BDSM anymore," she retorts. She knows she's pouting but she can't help it.

Jake laughs. "Bullshit. I'll bet if I bend you over and spank your stubborn arse you'll be begging me not to stop."

She crosses her arms in a show of defiance. "You're wrong, Jake. I'm no longer a submissive so get over it."

And now Jake was demanding that she submit again, or else. She opened her mouth, but remained mute. Her next words were crucial. *What should I do?*

"Jake…" She coughed nervously then tried again, "Jake. I'm not a sub anymore. What you're asking is unreasonable. But I do want to sort this out. I don't want to lose you."

"Bullshit." Jake's voice was angry, showing no sign of a compromise. "Of course you're still a sub, it's a part of who you are."

Frankie battled with her emotions as she tried to deny Jake's words. She'd truly believed she was a sub once so why didn't she feel that way now? She shrugged her shoulders and tried to hide the sense of hopelessness eating away at her.

"Look, all I'm asking is that you submit this weekend. I promise, I'll never ask it of you again if we decide to remain together." His voice was softer now as if he understood her dilemma.

Would he accept a vanilla relationship? She wasn't so sure. "But you're a Dom, Jake. You once said that vanilla sex doesn't turn you on." However she looked at it, there didn't seem to be an answer.

"That's immaterial right now. So, what's it to be, Frankie? You need to decide because we're due to meet Marco in forty minutes."

No, I won't do it. But to her astonishment, the words that came out of her mouth completely contradicted her thoughts.

"All right. I'll do it." *Jesus, did I really just say that?*

Jake's face lit up as he pulled her up into his arms and held her in a tight embrace.

"Oh, sweetie, thank you. You won't regret it, I promise." He buried his face in her hair and continued holding her. She savored the moment, having forgotten how good it felt to be held like that. When he pulled back, he traced her lips with his finger and whispered, "I love you."

Her eyes filled with tears and, as one escaped and ran down her cheek, he wiped it away with a gentle stroke. For the first time in almost two years, she welcomed the gesture and leaned into his comforting hand.

But it was when she looked up into his face that she realized, with shock, how his beautiful features bore the same shadows as hers. His eyes, before now a striking blue, were a little darker than before and the laughter lines around them now had the company of stress lines. How had she not noticed before? Maybe because she hadn't looked at him in a very long time. At least, not properly. His dark blond hair was still thick and immaculate, but was that a hint of gray at the temple?

Their eyes locked, as if they were both seeing the other for the first time. She was the first to break eye contact by lowering her gaze, fully aware of what the gesture implied, but it just seemed right. She gave him a shy smile and headed for the bathroom to get a quick shower before getting ready.

Half an hour later, she was standing in the same spot, showered and dressed in the tight leather dress Jake had discreetly packed without her noticing. Even in her high stiletto 'fuck me now' shoes, Jake towered over her, and she had to admit he looked sexy. He was wearing black leather trousers, black biker boots and a black leather waistcoat with nothing underneath. She'd forgotten how his muscles flexed across his broad shoulders when he moved and how his strong arms could pin her helplessly down with hardly any effort. He was still as fit and strong as he'd always been. She just hadn't noticed it recently.

But her earlier misgivings had returned and, even though Jake looked shit hot in his Dom's leathers, she was furious with herself for giving in so easily. Thank goodness none of her employees could see her now. How could she continue to demand the respect she'd worked so hard for if they saw her as this weak little woman, ready to hand complete control over to a man?

Oh fuck, what the hell have I agreed to? She opened her mouth to tell Jake she'd changed her mind, but at that same moment, his hand went to her right shoulder and pushed her gently downwards. "Kneel," he murmured.

Why did her knees turn to jelly at his command? Despite her intentions to tell him she'd changed her mind, she couldn't ignore the growing need between her legs that had intensified unbearably on hearing Jake order her to kneel. She didn't suppose it would hurt to play along for a little while longer so, with her heart hammering, she decided to obey him.

She had been so graceful at one time that she would have sunk smoothly to her knees without any effort. But now she balanced awkwardly on her heels as she tried to lower herself without toppling over. When she was finally on her knees in front of him, her emotions were raging from deep humiliation to a strange sense of well-being. She still battled with herself, though, reluctant to let go of the strong, assertive woman she'd become.

"Good girl."

His words sent a little shiver through her. How she'd loved to hear those words at one time.

"Look at me."

Heat burned her face as she slowly raised her head and looked into his eyes.

How could she ever have done this willingly? She met his gaze, expecting to see a look of triumph reflected in it, but to her surprise she saw only warmth and pleasure. She'd pleased him. A little flutter tickled her tummy and she felt herself relax some more.

Jake leaned over and picked something up from the table next to him. It was her old leather collar. A knot tightened in her throat as memories flooded back. She'd been so proud to wear that collar at one time.

Jake nodded at her and she instinctively lifted her hair, allowing him to fasten the collar around her neck. It felt so natural, so right. When the collar was secured, she let go of her hair and waited for Jake to allow her to stand again. It all seemed to be coming back with alarming ease.

"You look beautiful," he said, pulling her back up. "Now, I've been told there's no protocol during dinner but afterwards, we'll be taken to the dungeon—and I do believe it's a pretty impressive one—where the usual rules will apply."

Protocol? She hated protocol. She raised her eyebrows and tried not to scowl. "Are you telling me that I have to ask permission to speak?"

He nodded, solemnly.

"And I'm to call you *Sir*?" She practically spat the word 'sir' out.

"Definitely."

"Anything else? Will I have to crawl around on my hands and knees, naked, and kiss your feet in gratitude every time you acknowledge me?" The sarcasm in her voice actually made him smile. *Bastard!*

"No, but any insolence will be severely dealt with."

Despite her insistence that she was no longer into anything kinky, his words sent a little bolt of lightning through her body. She used to find it incredibly hot when Jake punished her. It had got to the point where he'd had to find other ways to discipline her because she'd enjoyed being spanked so much.

He'd been clever and inventive with his punishments and she had quickly learned not to be too sassy. She shuddered as she remembered only too well her frustration when he'd denied her an orgasm. She had practically screamed in frustration as he'd brought her to the brink and left her dangling—horny, desperate and needy as hell.

Jake turned to his black bag and took something else out, holding it behind his back so she couldn't see what it was. He had an impish grin on his face when he held up the leash he used to attach to her collar.

"No way," she cried. Oh God, the leash had always left her in no doubt as to Jake's control over her. It had been a powerful symbol of her submission and Jake knew it now, damn him.

"Come here." He pulled on the metal ring on her collar until she was directly in front of him again, then attached the leash. He now controlled her movements and the little butterflies in her stomach intensified. Damn it, she wouldn't enjoy this. She wouldn't!

Jake led her to the door, then stopped and turned to inspect her. Her face heated under his scrutiny and she couldn't help lowering her eyes submissively in response. God, what was wrong with her?

"That's my girl." He smiled and gently tugged on the leash as he led her down the long corridor toward the grand, sweeping staircase.

As they descended the stairs toward the sound of muffled voices the nervous butterflies in her belly ran amok. Someone was playing the piano, *Lakmé* by the sound of it. The beautiful, sensuous notes soothed her as Jake led her into the large entrance hall. Her eyes widened as the butler from earlier greeted them. He was now completely naked except for some sort of metal torture device clamped around his cock, and a thick, studded leather collar around his neck. He bowed and silently indicated that they should cross the hall and make their way down a long corridor. *This must be the East Wing.*

Her apprehension deepened as they walked along a wide corridor. She opened her mouth, ready to beg Jake to take her back up to their room, but he stopped and spoke before she had a chance to say anything.

"Do you remember your old safe word?"

Oh crap. Was she going to need her safe word tonight? She nodded slowly and whispered, "Mercy."

Jake looked satisfied and tugged on the leash. As they approached a high-arched oak door, someone stepped through it and came toward them with a broad smile on his face. Marco.

"Jake, I'm glad you could come." He and Jake gave each other a 'man hug' by slapping each other on the back before Marco turned his dark eyes on her. She shivered as she remembered the sting of his hand on her arse while Jake had watched nearby. That was a long time ago but, seeing him now, the memory was as fresh as if it had been yesterday. He still exuded power, which merged with his natural charm made him sexy as hell.

"Hello, beautiful," he said in his deep, gravelly voice. He took her hand and kissed her palm. "You're still as lovely as ever."

Frankie's cheeks burned as she looked up into Marco's rugged face. He was even taller than she remembered. His straight black hair wasn't quite as long as it had once been, but it was still wild and fell messily onto his broad shoulders. His strong jaw was covered with stubble, not long enough to be a beard but enough for him to look a bit like a highwayman, and his deep, intense eyes were still so dark that they looked almost black. They flashed with sparks of humor but also a hint of danger. He hadn't changed a bit.

Marco led them into a large drawing room, typical of a stately home except for the original paintings hanging on the walls. One was of a redhead, bent over a bench, her arse as red as the hair tumbling over her face. Another was of a beautiful dark-skinned submissive girl, kneeling in the slave position, wearing nothing but a silver collar around her neck.

There were probably about forty or fifty other people in the room, all mingling with glasses of champagne in their hands and smiles of anticipation on their faces. Several collared, naked girls glided gracefully around the guests, carrying trays of champagne. Frankie eyed the sparkling flutes and hoped one of the girls would come over soon. She needed a drink. Badly.

The fact that the people here were new to BDSM was oddly reassuring, knowing she wouldn't look out of place with her hesitance and clumsiness. She heard someone laugh and glanced across to the far end of the room. Cleo, the lady who had checked them in, was talking to a young couple. She looked stunning in a bright red rubber dress that clung to her perfect body. She had an air of self-assurance and confidence about her that Frankie envied and she self-consciously shifted from one foot to another, aware of her own awkwardness.

Finally, one of the naked girls approached them. Frankie smiled her thanks as the young woman offered her a glass of champagne. She quickly took a large gulp to help calm her nerves. The cool, sparkly liquid tickled her throat and she relaxed slightly as she watched the naked girls in fascination. Beautiful, elegant and clearly enjoying themselves, they seemed completely unfazed by their lack of clothing.

"These lovelies are my house slaves," said Marco fondly.

House slaves? *Shit*!

Jake laughed at her stunned reaction. "They're professional submissives, employed by Dominion."

"Oh." She took another large swig of her champagne and averted her eyes.

A young couple near them caught her attention and she tried not to look too obvious as she strained her ears to listen to what they were saying. They seemed to be having some sort of argument.

"For fuck's sake, Nick," hissed the girl, a deep frown etched on her pretty young face. "Just give it a go. Stop being such a fucking prude."

Frankie couldn't help smiling as she studied the young couple. He did look like a bit of a prude, actually. Clearly uncomfortable in his brand new fake leather trousers that didn't fit properly, he looked as if he would rather be at the dentist than in a BDSM hotel. He frowned as he took in his surroundings, his fingers clenched tightly around the glass in his hand. The girl, on the other hand, looked completely at home in a short leather micro skirt, a beautiful boned leather corset and bright red patent stiletto shoes. She was also studying her environment but, unlike her boyfriend, she had a look of excited anticipation on her face.

Frankie was so occupied watching the young couple that she wasn't aware Jake and Marco were talking to her until she noticed them both looking at her expectantly.

"What?" She took another large gulp of her champagne, which came back to haunt her when the bubbles forced a loud belch out of her. *Oh God, how embarrassing.*

"I was just telling Marco how wet you are at the prospect of playing in public again."

Not as embarrassing as that, though. Frankie opened her mouth to protest then shut it again quickly. To her shame, she realized that Jake was right. His words had somehow pushed that old magic button that she'd thought wasn't there anymore. The pulsing between her legs became almost painful as she imagined herself restrained and helpless, crying out as she was flogged in front of the crowd. She was damned if she was going to let Jake know that, though, and so glared obstinately back at him.

But Jake clearly wasn't going to let her off so easily. With an evil grin, he leaned down, patted her thighs to make her part them and thrust two fingers deep inside her, the way he always did when he wanted to prove a point.

Chapter Three

Jake almost cried with joy when he felt how wet Frankie's pussy was. Public play and humiliation had always been a favorite of hers and he'd been banking on that still being the case tonight. As he held his glistening fingers in front of Marco, his cock throbbed painfully inside the hot leather of his trousers. The urge to push her to her knees and have her suck it right there was almost overwhelming, but he knew he had to restrain himself. The night was still young.

Marco grinned at the sight of Jake's soaked fingers and winked at him. Jake had hinted to his old friend during their last chat how Frankie had lost interest in BDSM, although he hadn't revealed the true extent of their deteriorating relationship. Any doubt he'd had about Frankie's submissiveness were well and truly quashed now, though, and he felt a rush of pride for his wonderful wife as he watched her struggling with her emotions.

She was still his beautiful little slave girl. By the end of this weekend, not only did he hope they would be close again but, maybe, they could even resume their

D/s relationship. He mustn't get carried away, though. The last thing he wanted to do was spoil things by going too far, too soon. No, he'd take his time, gradually drawing his lovely subbie back to him.

He held his wet fingers under her nose, making her smell her arousal, and to his delight she opened her mouth slightly when he traced her lips. She closed her eyes as she sucked his fingers into her mouth, licking and tasting herself.

"Good girl," he whispered and withdrew his fingers. She looked almost disappointed at the loss.

Marco watched with a knowing smile. "Well, Jake, if you're still up for sharing your lovely wife, maybe we can have a little reunion in the dungeon later." His voice was husky, soft even.

A flush stained Frankie's cheeks and Jake knew the idea excited her. It excited him too. He hadn't dared to hope in his wildest dreams that Frankie would respond so beautifully tonight.

It was ironic that the idea of sharing his wife with his friend might help to save their marriage, when in a vanilla relationship something like that could very well split a couple up. But that was what he loved about BDSM—as long as it was safe, sane and consensual, pretty much anything went.

Marco excused himself then and turned his attention back to his other guests, leaving Frankie and Jake alone again.

"You okay?" he asked. He needed her to be okay with this. If there was any way she was truly struggling he would take her back upstairs immediately. The last thing he wanted to do was force her to do anything that would make her genuinely uncomfortable, but she really did seem to be taking it all in her stride.

Immense relief washed over him when she smiled and lowered her eyes. She probably wasn't aware of it yet, but she was still just as submissive as she'd always been. He just had to help remind her. And the fact that she hadn't kicked his balls to kingdom come by now was a good sign that he was slowly succeeding in his quest.

"Ladies and gentlemen. Welcome to Dominion." Marco's deep, gruff voice rang out across the room, and the hum of chatter hushed at once.

"Most of you here tonight are new to BDSM, and for you the purpose of this weekend is to help you decide if it really is for you. Some of you are here to rediscover the pleasures that this lifestyle can offer. Whatever the reasons you're here, you'll learn new things about yourselves that might shock you, but will ultimately enrich your lives. And, if you decide that kink isn't for you, at least you can finally lay the curiosity to rest.

"Dinner will be served shortly, and after that, you'll be shown to the dungeon where I'll be giving a rope bondage demonstration. You'll then be free to have a go yourselves, with the help of a Dungeon Monitor should you require it.

"Tomorrow morning, breakfast will be served from eight o'clock, which will be followed by a couple of workshops. After lunch, you'll be shown to the spa for some pampering and free time. We will reconvene down here at the same time for the second night of your introduction. Remember, the most fundamental rule of BDSM is safe, sane and consensual. If it's not consensual it's not BDSM, it's abuse. Don't ever forget that."

The murmur of agreement from the crowd seemed good enough for Marco and he gestured for them to go through to the dining room.

Jake tugged on Frankie's leash and they followed the crowd through an arched doorway. The dining room was magnificent, with beautifully carved cornices surrounding the high ceiling. An enormous marble hearth was at the center of one wall and floor-to-ceiling leaded windows let in the last of the early evening light.

The room was scattered with large round tables, each laid for about eight people, with crystal glasses and the finest porcelain plates set out in perfect symmetry. Shiny silver cutlery had been laid with military precision on crisp, starched white linen tablecloths. Tall silver candlesticks with thick, church-style candles and stunning vases, filled with lilies, decorated the center of each table, giving them a feeling of opulence and decadence. No expense had been spared by the look of it.

"Wow," whispered Frankie, as Jake led her to a board with the seating plan.

When he found their table, he unclipped Frankie's leash and held a chair for her to sit down. There was no one else at the table yet so he settled back to observe his beautiful wife as she fiddled with the stem of her champagne flute, still looking a little apprehensive. But her eyes were sparkling, something they hadn't done since the miscarriage and Jake felt quietly optimistic for their future as he studied her.

A movement in the corner of his eye made him drag his gaze off Frankie. Someone was approaching their table. A young couple, probably in their mid-twenties, were checking the name cards at the table. He had a vague memory of seeing them in the drawing room earlier, having some sort of argument. The girl was petite, blonde and very pretty but her partner was tall, lanky and seemed to have a permanent frown etched onto his face. They were an odd couple, not at all suited.

"Hello." The girl sat down next to Jake and grinned at them. "I'm Christina and this is Nick."

Nick nodded curtly but didn't say anything. The poor guy didn't look at all happy about being there, and Jake wondered if his girlfriend had dragged him there against his better judgment. A bit like he had done with Frankie. Guilt suddenly niggled at his conscience. Was Frankie still pissed off with him? Was she only going along with this because he hadn't given her any other choice? Of course she was. He was a bloody fool to think otherwise.

He turned to look at Frankie, but she was already introducing herself to Christina.

"And this is my husband, Jake," she said, smiling warmly.

He saw Christina eyeing Frankie's collar. "Are you already into this stuff?"

Frankie just shrugged and said, "We were, a long time ago. We're here this weekend to see if we still are."

"That's cool." Christina looked at her unsmiling boyfriend and scowled. "Nick thinks there's something wrong with me because I asked him to spank me. I'm hoping this weekend will change his mind."

"Not bloody likely," mumbled Nick under his breath.

Frankie gave Christina a sympathetic look just as another couple approached the table. Probably in her mid-forties, the woman looked very nervous as she found their name cards opposite Jake and Frankie. She looked across at them and smiled as she sat down.

"Good evening," said the woman in a soft voice, and they all smiled back at her.

Her sandy-colored hair had been styled into a classic chignon and her makeup matched the neat hairdo. Understated and modest. She had made an effort with her outfit, though. A shiny new black PVC dress hugged her figure, which, although not as lithe as it probably had been once, still looked sexy and toned.

The man looked only a little more at ease than she did. "Hello. My name's David and this is my wife, Sinead." David looked comfortable in his well-worn biker trousers and jacket.

Jake guessed that he probably belonged to a vintage biker club or something similar. He recognized a kindred spirit when he saw one and looked forward to asking David if he owned a motorbike later.

They all introduced themselves, except for Nick, who helped himself to a glass of water from the upmarket branded bottles that had been placed on the tables. Christina ignored him and wasted no time questioning everyone about their BDSM experience.

"So, have you done this before?" she quizzed. "I take it you're the Dom?" she asked David.

Sinead blushed as David answered, "Well, we're not really sure about all this yet. We recently celebrated our twenty-fifth wedding anniversary and thought we could do with spicing things up a bit in the bedroom. You know, now that the kids have left and all that." He coughed nervously, and his wife nodded her agreement.

"We've always wanted to try it, but it was just too impractical with kids in the house. We never had any privacy for a normal sex life let alone anything a bit kinky," said Sinead. She blushed again and quickly picked up a glass, before putting it hastily back when she saw that it was still empty.

"Well, you've come to the right place," said Christina with a giggle. "We're first-timers too."

"It's our first time here as well," said Frankie. "But we're not new to BDSM." She touched her collar subconsciously, as if it gave her reassurance. The gesture certainly gave Jake reassurance.

Jake sat back and watched Frankie as she chatted amiably with the two women. How was it that women could start talking as if they'd known each other for years, whilst the men just watched, sizing each other up? David seemed nice enough, but he didn't like the look of Nick. The younger man appeared just as miserable as he'd done when he'd first sat down, and Jake couldn't help feeling wary of him. Jake hoped the group wouldn't be forced into some hand-holding bonding session later, or something equally cringe-worthy — the only person he wanted to bond with was his wife.

He wondered who the last two places at the table were for. Hopefully, whoever they were had bottled it and wouldn't turn up now. The fewer strangers he had to make small talk with, the better.

He was both relieved and delighted when Marco and Cleo approached their table and sat down in the empty seats.

He grinned to himself as all three women blushed when he greeted them. Marco's power over the opposite sex was as strong as ever. Jake had yet to meet a woman who could resist Marco Alessi. Well, maybe Cleo, but as she was a Domme and Marco's oldest friend — she didn't count.

Cleo was the female equivalent of Marco — strong, sexy, dark and slightly dangerous. She and Marco had an unbreakable bond that had survived years of drama and trauma. They had never been lovers, though, as far as Jake was aware.

Marco was a firm and challenging Dom and was never short of willing submissives, but he was strictly one night only. He never got emotionally involved with any of his subs and rarely dated any of them.

"So, have you all been introduced?" asked Cleo, studying each guest carefully.

They all nodded and Christina replied, "Yes, we introduced ourselves."

"Good." Cleo's sharp eyes scanned the table again. "So, which of you cuties do I get to play with later?" Her eyes settled on Nick, who suddenly looked like he'd had a red hot chili shoved up his arse.

Jake suppressed a laugh. Cleo was incorrigible. She knew exactly what to say to get a reaction.

"You're more than welcome to have him," muttered Christina. "In fact, you can even keep him if you like."

Nick looked like he might explode, but remained obstinately silent, while Cleo turned her attention to Christina.

"Why, thank you, my dear. Although, he looks rather like a cat who ended up with sour milk instead of cream. Now you..." Cleo directed her words directly at Christina. "You look like the cream. Can I lick you up?"

Marco laughed and slapped the back of Cleo's hand. "Behave yourself."

"If I must," said Cleo, with a good-natured shrug.

"Please excuse my business partner," said Marco, and grinned at Christina. "Her bark's far worse than her bite."

Christina, to her credit, licked her lips. "Please don't apologize. She can bite me any time."

Everyone around the table laughed, except for Nick, who now looked like he was about to implode.

Cleo winked at Christina across the table and said in a low, sexy voice, "I'll see you in the dungeon later."

Jake glanced at Marco, who grinned. *This should be a very interesting evening.*

With the ice broken, they all relaxed and got to know each other better as the house slaves served the wine. He learned that David and Sinead hadn't had sex in over a year and that this weekend was their way of rekindling what had once been a very passionate sex life.

Christina and Frankie seemed to have hit it off and quickly found common ground when they discovered they both worked in marketing. He knew Frankie would enjoy Christina's uncomplicated and easy-going manner, and was happy to see his wife looking more relaxed than she had in a long time.

Marco raised his glass. "Cheers, everyone, and welcome."

The slaves, now dressed in little black and white latex maid outfits brought steaming bowls of lobster bisque and warm, crusty bread rolls. The meal was delicious, the company relaxed and entertaining. Even Nick managed a smile of sorts when Marco and Cleo had a lively debate on which paddles left the best bruises.

Halfway through the meal, Marco leaned toward him and spoke quietly in his ear, "Hey, old buddy. Would you have any objections if I borrowed Frankie for the Shibari demo later?"

Jake grinned back at his old friend. He knew Frankie would openly object and appear mortified by being the star attraction in the dungeon, but he also knew she had a soft spot for Marco—and that, along with her enjoyment of playing in public, would be more than she would be able to resist.

He watched his wife chatting happily with Christina, so comfortable in her collar that she appeared to have forgotten she was wearing it, and knew she would be fine with it. What better way to remind her of her natural submissiveness than to be publicly bound in rope by Marco? With an excited grin on his face, he nodded at Marco and said, "Be my guest."

Chapter Four

Frankie smiled and thanked Marco as he refilled her wine glass. They'd just finished dessert and were waiting for coffee to be served. Cleo was telling Jake about a guy who made the most incredible wooden St. Andrew's Crosses and, more worryingly, where he could purchase one, and the other guests around the table were engrossed in their own chat. Well, except for Nick, who had hardly spoken a word since they'd arrived. She wondered why on earth he'd agreed to come if he was so against it. At least she hadn't known what Jake had had in mind when he'd brought her here, but apparently Nick had agreed, knowing what was in store.

Cleo's husky laughter brought her attention back to Marco's friend and business partner. She was probably in her mid-thirties and was stunningly beautiful. Her fiery red hair matched the red gloss on her lips and her eyes were the color of deep emeralds. Beautifully crafted tattoos graced the skin on her arms and back, as if they were works of art painted on the finest canvas. Several piercings on her face and body told Frankie that Cleo wasn't afraid of a bit of pain. It was ironic really—she herself got off on erotic pain and yet the idea of a needle piercing any part of her body made her eyes water with horror. On the other hand, as a Domme and sadist, Cleo enjoyed inflicting pain on someone else, but clearly wasn't a lightweight when it came to experiencing it herself either.

"So, how come I haven't met Cleo before?" she asked, turning to face Marco.

Marco smiled. "She was always on the move around the time I met you. As well as being the manager of our band, she was the bassist in a very successful female rock group." He paused a moment, his expression becoming serious, then he said, "Anyway, enough about Cleo. How about you? I told Jake when we met up again how worried I'd been that I hadn't heard from you both for so long and he told me about the baby. I'm so sorry."

Frankie's heart tightened painfully at his words and tears stung her eyes that she furiously forced back. She wasn't about to lose control now. As if sensing her pain, Marco took hold of her hand and gave it a squeeze.

"I can't imagine what you must have gone through." His voice was gentle. Very few people had ever heard that tone and her tears hovered dangerously on the brink as memories returned to tear at her soul. Would the pain ever go away?

"Don't worry, I'll change the subject." Marco's eyes, usually so dark and hard, were soft as he smiled kindly at her.

She smiled shakily back to let him know that a change of subject would be greatly appreciated. Marco was a good man, scary when he went all Dom-like, but she trusted him and appreciated the rare moments that he showed his softer side. Jake and Marco had known each other for years, but Frankie hadn't actually met Marco until her wedding day. When she'd learned that Jake's old school friend had planned his tour dates around their wedding, she'd been flattered and curious to meet this famous friend who she'd heard so much about. Now she considered him almost as good a friend as Jake did. She felt bad that neither she nor Jake had returned any of his calls over the last couple of years.

"When I bumped into Jake and invited you both here, he said something about you not being into kink anymore. Of course, I laughed and told him not to be so stupid." The gentleness was gone again, now replaced with the stern tone of a Dom who expected a straight answer.

"I..." How could she explain it? She didn't even understand it herself. She had been so sure that she wasn't into BDSM anymore, yet here she was wearing a collar and dining with a room full of kinksters, and she didn't actually feel out of place at all. In fact, she felt disturbingly comfortable surrounded by these people, who liked their sex with a little added spice.

"Frankie," said Marco, quietly. "You are probably the most naturally submissive person I've ever met. I don't mean generally. You're still the feisty, independent and assertive woman you always were, but sexually? Well, let me ask you a question — If Jake ordered you over his knee for a spanking right now, in front of everyone here, how would you feel?"

She blushed as she imagined the scenario and her pulse quickened as the thought turned her on more than she cared to admit. *Damn!*

Before she could think of a reply, Marco answered for her, "You'd hump his fucking leg to get him to hit you harder. And then you'd drop to your knees and beg to suck his cock."

Marco had always been blunt, but she'd forgotten just how much. Her pussy smoldered as Marco's words taunted her. He was right, of course, but she couldn't admit that to him.

His dark eyes didn't miss a thing, though, and she realized she didn't have to say anything. He knew.

"Tell me I'm right," he whispered, coarsely.

She shook her head vigorously. "No. No, I'm not like that anymore."

But Marco just laughed. "Really? We'll see later, shall we? By the way, Jake has agreed to loan you out to me for the Shibari demo later. I seem to remember you're rather partial to being bound in rope."

The arousal instantly drained out of her and was replaced with an angry fire burning in her gut. How dare Jake agree to that without checking with her first? She opened her mouth to tell Marco that he could get lost, but he took a firm hold of her chin and forced her to meet his steely gaze. "Don't fight it. Let go and enjoy it," he growled. "Remember, you can always use your safe word. Do you want to use your safe word, Frankie?"

He was right. All she had to do was say the word. But was that what she really wanted? Her clitoris ached at the prospect of being used in public by both Jake and Marco. Shit, she wanted this. Slowly, she shook her head and whispered, "No."

Marco nodded, satisfied that he'd made his point. "Now, if you'll excuse me, I need to talk to a couple of people before we make our way to the dungeon." He leaned over and kissed her on the cheek. "I'll see you later." The promise of dark delights to come hung heavily in his words, and her cheeks burned with shame at the effect they had on her.

As Marco rose, Jake turned to her and smiled. "Everything okay?"

She glared back at him. "Well, apart from the fact you've told Marco he can tie me up in front of all the bloody guests, yes, I'm fine."

She watched in satisfaction as a worried frown crossed his face but then softened when she saw his genuine concern.

"I thought you'd enjoy it," he said, with a sheepish look on his face. "But, if you really don't want to..."

"It's okay. I've told Marco I'll do it." She smiled, wanting him to know that it really was okay, and she felt comforted by the admiration reflected back in his eyes. As she stared at him she suddenly found it impossible to look away and break the intent gaze that held her trapped like a prisoner. Or like a restrained submissive. She couldn't suppress the little shiver that ran through her body and she knew he'd seen it when his pupils dilated slightly in response.

Marco's voice brought their attention back to the dining room and they reluctantly tore their eyes away from each other as it was announced there would be a little light after-dinner entertainment to get everyone in the mood for later. This turned out to be one of the house slave's punishments for not serving as well as the other slaves. The pretty brunette was told to lay herself across a bench, face down, then she was strapped securely onto it so she couldn't move. Her legs were spread wide and the angle in which she lay made her arse jut nicely upwards. Frankie felt a stirring of arousal as she remembered being restrained just like that a long time ago.

A volunteer was then asked to bring the slave to multiple orgasms with a vibrating wand that looked like a giant microphone, but was so powerful it could induce earth-shattering orgasms in no time at all. Jake had used it on Frankie for forced orgasms and she had always succumbed, screaming in a mixture of ecstasy and agony. It was one of her favorite yet most hated toys.

Needless to say, there was no shortage of volunteers. A tall, muscular man covered in tattoos grinned as he was given the wand. The crowd laughed when he gave the slave a light smack directly on her pussy before placing the wand on her clit. He must have turned the dial straight to 'high' as the loud buzzing noise was clearly audible. Marco, standing next to the slave with a thin cane in his hand, laughed and chatted to his guests as the poor slave started whimpering at the effects of the wand. Frankie squirmed in her seat as she recalled exactly how that felt.

As the slave became more excited, Marco started landing light taps of the cane on her arse, not hard enough to leave marks, but enough to make the slave groan louder. Then, just as her body gave the telltale shudder of orgasm, Marco sliced the cane through the air and hit her hard across the buttocks. The slave screamed and came so hard it looked like she might break free of the restraints.

"Leave the wand on her clit," ordered Marco to the volunteer, who grinned in agreement.

Frankie's eyes watered with sympathy. Within seconds the slave's body started shuddering again and, like before, just as she was about to come, Marco landed another hard hit of the cane across her arse. The combination of the intense pain mingling with the overwhelming pleasure was obvious, and Frankie actually felt envious of the girl on the bench while she was made to come again and again.

When the slave's backside was marked with several equally placed dark red stripes, Marco told the volunteer to stop, and Marco released her from the bench. The girl's eyes were glassy as she tried to steady herself, and when she was led out of the room for some aftercare, everyone applauded.

"Now that's what I call after-dinner entertainment," laughed one guest.

"There's plenty more where that came from," said Marco, with a discreet look in Frankie's direction, then invited his guests to make their way to the dungeon for their introduction to the wonderful world of kink.

"Wow, that was hot," said Christina, sounding breathless, as she rose from her seat. Her cheeks were pink and her eyes wide—she'd obviously found the whole scene very erotic. As had Frankie.

Frankie grinned at her and leaned over to whisper in Christina's ear, "Well, you never know, maybe it had an effect on Nick."

"Oh, it had an effect all right. He says he wants to leave." Christina straightened her shoulders, as if coming to a decision. "In fact, do you know what? Let him fucking leave. But he'll be leaving alone, I'm not going anywhere."

Frankie frowned. "But it's strictly couples only tonight, isn't it?"

Christina's face fell, and her disappointment pulled at Frankie's heart. It was clear that she was desperate to stay and had probably had to work very hard to convince Nick to even come along tonight. But she couldn't blame Nick for wanting to leave. BDSM wasn't for everyone and Christina had to respect that.

The same thought must have occurred to Christina because her eyes filled with tears as her dream was about to come to an abrupt end.

"Let me have a word with Marco," whispered Frankie, "I can't promise anything, but you do, after all, have a date with Cleo in the dungeon later. It would be rude not to show up."

Christina's face lit up. "Thank you," she cried, "I'd really appreciate that."

"In the meantime, go and talk to Nick. Remember, you can't blame him for not wanting to do this. It's got to be consensual on both sides." Frankie gave the young girl a stern look before crossing the room to find Marco. He was with Cleo, which could work to Christina's advantage. Cleo had clearly taken to the young novice and it would be in her interest to help convince Marco to let her stay.

"Hi." She flashed them both a broad smile and waited for Marco to ask her if everything was all right.

But instead he growled, "Where's your Master?"

Marco's frown caught her breath and made her suck in a gulp of air. But, despite Marco's commanding presence, and the fact that he owned the place, Frankie scowled at his words. That was not how she had anticipated the conversation would start.

She tried to stamp on the flash of defiance that surfaced, but to no avail. "He's not my Master, and anyway, even if he was, I don't have to follow him around like a fucking puppy." Oh crap, what had she done? She seemed to remember that Marco came down hard on subs who answered back.

To confirm her fears, Marco's eyes narrowed. "Frankie, for your information, now that dinner is finished I expect you to follow protocol, so, yes, you do have to follow him around like a puppy." His voice was low, dangerous, but Frankie stood her ground.

"Marco, for *your* information, Jake has gone to the gents. I do believe that you don't permit females in there?" She placed her hands on her hips and glared angrily back at him. *Oh fuck, I'm so going to pay for that later.*

Marco's face looked like a black thundercloud about to explode with an almighty clap at any moment. Cleo looked on, clearly interested to see how far this brat could push Marco. There was a moment, a very long, silent moment, where they just glared at each other. Frankie wasn't going to back down, though. She might be submissive when it came to sex, but she'd be damned if she'd let anyone tell her what to do outside the fucking bedroom. Or rather, in this case, outside the dungeon.

The moment seemed to last forever then, suddenly, a loud boom told her that the thundercloud had finally exploded. Thankfully, the sound that reached her ears wasn't rage, but laughter. "Oh, Frankie, my dear, you haven't changed a bit. You're still the same sassy brat you were before. I can see that Jake is going to have his work cut out retraining you."

Frankie glanced at Cleo, who grinned back at her and suddenly all three of them were laughing.

"Sorry about that," giggled Frankie, as Jake returned to claim her. "I guess it's been a while since anyone told me what to do."

"Uh-oh. What's she done?" asked Jake, giving her a look of dread.

"She's been rude, sassy and disobedient," said Marco, with a good-natured smirk.

"That's my girl." Jake squeezed her shoulder, and Frankie thought for a moment that Jake was actually condoning her behavior. Until he said, "I knew it wouldn't be long before you earned your first punishment."

At the word 'punishment' her stomach hit the floor then bounced back up and hit her hard between the legs. She actually had to hold onto Jake to steady herself, as a massive wave of lust weakened her knees. Somehow, his words had just pushed her into that beautiful melty headspace of submission and she struggled for a moment to remember why she'd sought Marco out in the first place. *Oh yes, Christina.*

"Marco. Sir. Master Marco," she uttered, demurely. *Might as well cover all bases.* "May I ask a favor, please?"

Cleo laughed. "Hell, Marco, we're not even in the dungeon yet and she's already asking for favors."

Frankie looked at Cleo and smiled. "Actually, it involves you, too."

"Whatever it is, the answer is yes," purred Cleo. "My, you really are quite irresistible, aren't you?"

"Hands off, Cleo. She's mine." Jake's retort set both Cleo and Marco off again, and Frankie decided to use their good humor to her advantage.

"Christina—the young girl at our table—has had a bit of a setback. It seems her partner wants to leave but—"

Before she had the chance to continue, Marco interrupted her, "Frankie, you know it's strictly couples only this weekend. Apart from the house slaves, who are employed by me, no single people are allowed."

"But..." Damn, she wasn't going to give in that easily. She turned to Cleo and gave the Domme her sexiest smile. "She was so looking forward to your expert tutelage, Cleo. Please let her stay, this means so much to her."

Frankie watched as Cleo gave Marco an inquisitive look. They were considering it. Good, now all she had to do was play her trump card. "She's going to explore BDSM regardless, and if you don't let her stay here, she'll go to some dodgy club and risk her safety by hooking up with a potentially dangerous thug posing as a Dom."

She knew Marco was fiercely protective of his subs and prayed that her tactic would work. She held her breath as she watched Cleo raise her eyebrows at him and finally, he nodded. "All right. But she's your responsibility, Cleo."

Frankie couldn't help reaching up on tiptoes and kissing Marco on his cheek. "Thank you."

He rolled his eyes and grinned. "Tell the girl to come and see me straight away."

Before she could go, though, Jake grabbed her arm and pulled her close. "You may go and find Christina," he growled, clearly reminding her that he was in control, "then I need to see you alone before you become Marco's puppet. There's a matter of your punishment to deal with."

It was all she could do not to sink to her knees there and then. Damn Jake. The word 'punishment' acted as a kind of trigger that sent her into deep submissive arousal. With her stomach clenching in almost unbearable excitement, she waited as Jake refastened the leash to her collar. Every bit of defiance and deluded denial drained out of her as she bowed her head and whispered, "Yes, Master."

Chapter Five

Holy fuck, she'd called him Master. Jake turned away from Frankie so she wouldn't see the glassy emotion that must surely be pouring out of his eyes. It wouldn't do for her to see the soft side of him right now. She wanted the strict, stern Dom who would forcefully throw her over his knee and blister her arse with hard, relentless spanks.

He'd enjoy dishing out the first spanking he'd given in years, although, of course, it wouldn't be a real punishment. More like a *funishment*. Erotic spankings had always been a favorite of theirs and his hand itched with horny anticipation as he imagined her squirming on his knee.

He loved the way she couldn't resist a punishment. But it had admittedly become a bit of a problem when he'd realized that she'd been deliberately provoking him. As a Dom, he wouldn't tolerate certain behavior, like disobedience or disrespect, and he'd had to find new ways to punish her that didn't actually reward her. She'd been seriously pissed off the first time he'd denied her an orgasm. It had worked, though.

When Frankie returned from giving Christina the good news, he took hold of her leash again and gave it a firm tug.

"Come here," he ordered, not giving her much choice as he led her toward a large chair in the middle of the room. Leaving her standing awkwardly in front of him, he sat himself down and patted his leather-clad lap. Frankie's cheeks glowed red as long buried memories were undoubtedly resurfacing, but she hesitated only briefly before stepping tentatively toward him.

His excitement heightened as he reached up, grabbed her hand and pulled her roughly down over his lap. As he did so, he couldn't help groaning as her weight pressed against his growing erection. God she felt good splayed across his lap—he'd so missed this. She wriggled, trying to balance herself, and he placed one hand firmly on her back, pressing her down to keep her in place.

"Jake—"

"Tell me how much you've missed being spanked," he interrupted. He smiled to himself as he felt her stiffen in denial and pressed harder down on her back in response. He knew how much she loved being restrained, even held in place like this, and he guessed she'd probably be cursing him right now for putting her into yet more conflict with herself.

When she didn't respond, he reached up and grabbed a fistful of her hair. Yanking it just hard enough to get her attention he said, "Tell me, Frankie."

"Damn you, Jake." Her voice was raspy, heavy with emotion. And desire. He knew her so well.

Giving her hair another tug, he lowered his voice, sounding just dangerous enough to be threatening, "I won't ask again. Tell me how you feel. How you've missed lying across my lap like this, waiting for my hand to spank your pretty little arse."

She groaned. He had her. Sure enough, a second later, she cried her reply, "Okay. I've missed you spanking me. Okay?"

"Try again."

Was that a growl that had just escaped from her throat? Grinning, he waited for her response.

"I've missed you spanking me, *Sir*."

"Good. Tell me how much you want me to spank you right now, Frankie." As he spoke, he rubbed his free hand over the soft contours of her bottom, pressing sexily against the tight leather of her dress.

"I'd really like you to spank me, Sir." Her voice was barely audible, a sure sign that she was getting closer to the submissive headspace he so loved her to be in. Her inner struggle was nearly over.

"Are you begging, Frankie?" This was the test. If she wasn't quite there yet, she'd probably jump off his lap and thump him.

But, she remained still and quietly whimpered. "Yes, Sir. I'm begging. Please spank me."

"Why?" He didn't want to push his luck, but he just couldn't help taking her a little further.

"Because I've been a bad girl, Sir. And because it pleases you."

His erection took on a new dimension as it throbbed painfully under Frankie's weight. Hearing her utter those words caused the blood in his cock to pound so hard that he thought he might explode at any minute. *Down boy*, he urged himself. Control had always been one of his strengths and he intended it to remain that way.

To give himself a moment to recover, he stroked Frankie's thighs then lifted her skirt, exposing her gorgeous bare bottom. She groaned, maybe from momentary embarrassment, then her body visibly relaxed again on his lap. She was surrendering, he knew the signs. And he hadn't even smacked her yet.

He tried to swallow the lump in his throat as he gently rubbed Frankie's arse. The skin was smooth and pale with not a single blemish anywhere. He was about to remedy that.

He lifted his hand then brought it back down, hard. She squealed as the first slap echoed in the nearly empty room. Most people had made their way through to the dungeon, but the few who still remained turned at the unmistakable sound. He knew they now had a small audience and he didn't hesitate in letting Frankie know.

"They're watching us, Frankie," he whispered. "They're watching you take your punishment for being such a naughty girl."

He touched her between her legs, brushing his finger softly against her smooth labia and when it made contact with her wetness he knew his words had just added impact to that first hit. He slapped her arse even harder, again and again.

He watched in fascination as the skin on her buttocks started to turn pink. When she squirmed her body rubbed against his cock and he gradually allowed himself to be drawn into Frankie's world of pleasure. He could almost feel the burn on her arse, the buzz it was giving her as he continued to rain his relentless slaps down on her.

"Oh," she cried, as she tried to bring her legs up.

He pushed them firmly down again and continued spanking her. His hand was stinging now. She wouldn't know it, but it was almost as sore as her arse must be. It felt good. But next time he'd use a paddle or even her hairbrush.

After a while he felt Frankie's body go limp and he slowed down his assault. He rubbed her glowing-red globes, feeling the heat radiating off them. He wanted to soothe her now, bring her back down as gently as possible. So he massaged her burning skin with feathery strokes while he continued to hold her in place with a firm grip.

"Frankie?" His voice sounded disembodied, like it didn't belong to him. She wasn't the only one who'd been affected by this.

"Hmm?"

"Sit up, beautiful."

He pulled her up and lifted her so she was sitting on his lap, careful not to put too much pressure on her sore backside. He reached his arms protectively around her shivering body and held her close. Aftercare had always been a favorite of his — it was a chance to feel the closeness between them as Frankie slowly recovered from whatever he'd dished out.

She lowered her head so that it was resting on his shoulder, and he savored the feel of her panting against his neck. For the first time in almost two years, he felt at peace and his heart contracted as his love for his beautiful wife reasserted itself.

He closed his eyes as she relaxed into him, and caught a hint of her lemon-scented soap. So familiar. So Frankie. God, this felt good. She was so close to him that he could feel the pulse in her neck and the heavy thumping of her heart against his chest. He pulled her even closer and took a deep breath. *Mine.* As he thought it, he experienced an overpowering feeling of gratitude and humility. *She's mine and there's no way I'm going to let her go.*

The strength of his love hadn't diminished in response to her recent aloofness. He chuckled. There was nothing aloof about her now, snuggled close to him, her body fitting perfectly against his own. The first barrier was down. It looked like his plan might be working. By the end of this weekend, it was very possible that they could have saved their marriage.

They must have remained in the same position for another ten minutes or so. Then Frankie stretched on his lap, and he opened his eyes to find himself staring into her dazed eyes.

"Hello," he said, with a grin. "Welcome back."

She smiled up at him, looking a bit like a stoned hippy. "Hello." Her voice was croaky and oh so sexy.

He glanced over her shoulder and established that they were alone — their audience had long gone.

A thin lock of her hair was hanging over her right eye and he couldn't resist the urge to gently tuck it behind her ear.

"Hmm. I've missed this," he murmured, stroking the soft skin on the inside of her thigh.

She tensed a little, but remained silent.

"I don't mean the spanking. Well, I do, but I didn't mean that just now. I meant that I've missed this closeness between us."

"Jake, don't."

He frowned. "What?"

"Let's not get too deep right now. I know we need to talk, and we will, but not now. Why don't we just enjoy ourselves tonight and we'll talk in the morning?" Her voice was calm, her guard down. He knew she meant it. That was good enough.

"Okay." He kissed her hard, savoring her sweet taste. When he pulled away again, he brushed her cheek with the back of his fingers and stared into her eyes. "I love you so much, Frankie. I'll do whatever it takes not to lose you."

She smiled. "I think I've worked that out by now. You won't lose me. I love you and want to sort things out as much as you do."

This time he couldn't mask the tears that momentarily blurred his vision. That was all he'd wanted to hear. She loved him. Happiness bubbled up inside him and he pulled her close again. When he let her go, he tipped her off his lap, swatted her backside with a playful slap, then said, "Now, get your arse down to that dungeon."

As they headed down a corridor leading to the dungeon, Frankie enjoyed the lingering warmth on her bottom. Despite her earlier feelings of both defiance and humiliation, she'd enjoyed her so-called punishment. And it wasn't just the spanking. She grudgingly acknowledged the fact that she had derived great pleasure from knowing she'd pleased Jake. So why did she still have a little niggle of uncertainty?

And there was the pain. She'd forgotten that in order to get the intense pleasure, she first had to work through the pain. And it had hurt. As her skin had warmed with each hit, the sting had become stronger until she'd wondered if she could take any more. But, oddly, that had only made her want more. Jake had a strong hand—he knew how to spank—and there had been no escaping the relentless blows. She'd fought it at first, like she always did, but then everything had come together and it had all made sense. The pain, followed by the surrender, had led to the pleasure. A pleasure so overwhelming that she hadn't ever wanted it to end.

She didn't recall it actually ending. The only thing she remembered now was snuggling into Jake as he'd held her in his strong arms. The way he always did after a scene. He might be an uncompromising Dom, but he always looked after her. Cared for her.

Sometimes, though, he could get a bit too intense, and she'd sensed that might have been the case while she'd been sitting on his lap just then. But the time hadn't been right.

She knew they were nearly at the dungeon when the sexy slap of leather hitting naked skin reached her ears. She'd forgotten how the sound and smell of a dungeon added to the erotic atmosphere and her heart beat a little faster as they approached a big, heavy oak door propped open with a cast iron statue of a naked woman.

Sure enough, the scent of leather and rubber reawakened familiar senses, but the smell of sweat and sex was notably absent. The noises were more subdued as well. Normally, they'd be greeted by groans, even screams, combined with gasps of pleasure in response to leather meeting flesh. Here, though, the only thing she could hear now that the sexy slaps of impact play had stopped was subdued music, low voices and nervous giggles. It seemed the flogger she'd heard a moment ago had come from a Dungeon Monitor giving a young couple a quick demonstration.

She sighed, trying to hide any outward signs of disappointment. This wasn't quite what she'd been expecting. Then she remembered it was beginners' night and her mood lightened at the sight of the apprehensive newbies tentatively trying out the equipment. The atmosphere would heat up soon enough – she knew from experience that the awkwardness amongst the guests wouldn't last long.

"Hey, you two, I wondered where you'd got to." Christina tottered up to them, and Frankie smiled at the excitement on her face.

Jake answered with a grin. "We had a matter of some firm discipline to sort out." He playfully stroked Frankie's arse, still warm from earlier, then gently tapped it to make his point. "I think she's remembered her place."

Before Frankie could think of a smart reply, Christina giggled and said, "Ooh, Frankie, you're so lucky. What I wouldn't give for a bit of discipline right now."

Frankie couldn't help smiling. Cleo had approached Christina from behind and was listening without the young girl knowing. When Christina opened her mouth to add something, Cleo reached out and tugged on Christina's hair, pulling her head gently back. Then, she put her glossy lips against Christina's ear and whispered, just loud enough for Frankie to hear, "You, young lady, will get more discipline tonight that you ever dared hope for. In fact, you may even regret those words later."

Christina's cheeks reddened and her pupils dilated – the rush of adrenaline evident on her flushed face. Cleo winked at Frankie and Jake then said, "Now, if you'll excuse us." Cleo, still holding onto Christina's hair, then marched the girl across the room, toward a St. Andrew's Cross.

Jake chuckled. "I think your young friend might be about to get her first lesson in bondage and discipline."

Frankie laughed as the formidable Domme strapped Christina's wrists to the top arms of the cross.

"Come on." Jake tugged on Frankie's leash and led her over to a plush-looking sofa. "I should be making you crawl on your hands and knees now that we're in the dungeon. You see how nice I can be by letting you walk?"

Although he was smiling, Frankie didn't miss the underlying reminder in his voice that she was his submissive and that she'd better not forget it. She wasn't quite sure how she felt about that.

She didn't reply, just lowered her head and waited for him to indicate that she could sit down. She half expected him to have her kneel on the floor by his feet, but he must have been feeling generous as he gallantly allowed her to sit on the sofa next to him.

She sat back and looked around her. This was unlike any dungeon she'd ever seen. There were no black or red painted walls or fake stone cladding, no theme areas, no dance floor or loud music and no fake medieval light fittings. But there was still no doubting the purpose of the large, airy space. Not unlike the drawing room, large original paintings of beautiful submissive girls graced the patterned walls. Gold and burgundy crests were embossed on silky wallpaper, giving the dungeon an almost regal feel. The carpet, rather than being sticky and stained, was thick and plush and the same deep shade of burgundy as the crests on the wall. Crystal chandeliers hung from the high ceiling, making it feel more like a small ballroom than a dungeon.

But there was no mistaking it was a dungeon. Two tall St. Andrew's Crosses, several different-shaped spanking benches, a cage and a wall full of whips, floggers and paddles left her in no doubt about that.

There was a small stage to the right and a wicked looking bondage chair next to it.

Mmm. She's restrained in a chair, her nipples hard and her skin shivering. Leather straps are keeping her legs spread open leaving her exposed and vulnerable.

She smiled at the memory—she'd been given four glorious orgasms in that chair.

In an effort to calm her speeding pulse, she dragged her eyes away from the chair and continued looking around her. A pair of thick leather cuffs attached to chains dangled close to where they were sitting. The chains were attached to a mechanical hoist that would allow the cuffs to be raised and lowered accordingly. Frankie couldn't help imagining herself stretched and helpless in the cuffs as she waited for the bite of a heavy flogger. The shiver that ran through her body at the thought left little goosebumps on her arms and her stomach fluttered in anticipation.

Jake pulled her close and she snuggled into him, enjoying the opportunity for a cuddle whilst continuing to assess her surroundings. The sofa they were sitting on was just one of many, along with several large Queen Anne style armchairs and a red leather chaise longue in the far corner. This place was clearly designed for comfort and opulence as well as kinky, decadent play, and the combination was unusual and refreshing. The fifty or so people there were just enough to give it an atmosphere of erotic anticipation without it feeling crowded.

A tattooed man nearby pulled his male sub over a spanking bench and the first slap of a spanking echoed around the room. It shouldn't take too long for things to warm up. Excitement tingled through Frankie's body at the thought.

A woman nearby reminded her of when Jake had first introduced her to the scene. The woman was around the same age as she'd been and didn't look at all comfortable in her high stilettos and shiny PVC dress.

"You won't leave me alone, will you?" she asked her partner in a jittery voice. She looked very nervous, just like Frankie herself had been. That seemed like such a long time ago now.

"It's important to check that the bonds aren't too tight."

She looked away from the nervous woman toward the sound of the voice that had just spoken. Sinead was strapped onto a spanking bench while a Dungeon Monitor emphasized a few safety points to David.

Nearby a couple were trying to work out what the strange-looking contraption was in front of them. It was a leather padded bench and had a mechanical device at one end with a dildo attached. Frankie smiled at their baffled faces. They would undoubtedly discover it was a fucking machine in good time.

One of the house slaves approached, bowed to Jake and listened silently as Jake asked for two glasses of sparkling water. When the naked girl scurried off to fetch their drinks, Frankie turned to Jake and frowned.

"Water?" She had been hoping for more champagne.

"You've had enough alcohol. It's going to be a long night and I want you to keep a clear head. Trust me, you're going to need it." The tone in Jake's voice held no joviality.

Christ, he's serious.

She didn't reply—she might say something that would get her into trouble so it was probably best to remain silent. The conflicting emotions she'd felt earlier returned and her body tensed. Now that most of the euphoria of her spanking had diminished, her stubborn and assertive mind was beginning to break through again.

Her irritation at not getting another glass of champagne was exacerbated by the fact that she didn't have the control to make the decision for herself. Rationally she knew Jake had her best interests at heart. BDSM and alcohol didn't mix. When she got drunk, she got sleepy and her body didn't respond as normal. Her pain threshold was temporarily distorted and she would more than likely forget to call her safe word if things got too much. She knew that, but damn him, she wanted another drink right now.

"Why are you scowling?" Jake never missed a thing and, as a Dom, never let her get away with anything. She couldn't even hide her fucking facial expressions so she had at least a small bit of privacy. The irritation deepened.

"I'm not scowling," she snapped.

Then the bastard laughed, fueling her annoyance.

"Are you sulking because I ordered water for you?" Jake clearly thought this was funny and, in response, a little more submissiveness seeped out of her as she clenched her fists.

Leave it, Frankie. Don't vex him. But, although the intelligent part of her brain knew it would be foolish to open her mouth at this point, the reckless part won and she just couldn't help herself as she spat, "No, but when I get that fucking water, you're going to be wearing it."

Her heart sank as Jake's face darkened. *Why the hell did I say that?* The one thing she remembered only too well from their previous D/s relationship was that Jake never tolerated rudeness. Her punishments had been harsh, beyond depriving her of the odd orgasm.

The cane he'd kept for such purposes was vicious and left her in no doubt as to the difference between a real punishment and an erotic one. By the glare in Jake's eyes now, she knew she'd crossed the line and she was going to pay for it.

Chapter Six

Frankie closed her eyes in the hope that when she opened them again, Jake would have vanished. But no such luck. As she peeped out from behind her eyelashes, her stomach clenched with dread when his brows narrowed as his eyes hardened.

Before she had a chance to laugh and pretend it had been a joke, a low guttural growl emanated from him and he pushed her firmly off the sofa.

"Kneel, arms behind your back and forehead against the floor. *Now!*" Although his voice was controlled, the ice beneath the words made his displeasure clear, but Frankie was too shocked by his order to be concerned about what Jake might be feeling. He wanted her on the floor? She knew the position he demanded was about as submissive as you could get. It would be obvious to the other guests what was going on. Everyone would know she was being punished, but this wasn't the sort of public humiliation she got off on. This was real and genuinely shameful.

Her flaming cheeks, though, were more from trying to keep her temper in line than from remorse. The temptation to tell Jake to get stuffed was overwhelming. Still crouching on the floor where he'd pushed her off the sofa, she fought to regain some control. Balancing herself on her knees, she crossed her arms mutinously to show him that she wasn't going to tolerate being pushed around like that. Then she flashed him a 'How dare you?' glare and raised her chin in defiance.

But the look she got back sent a chill through to her core. Rather than the anger she'd been expecting to see, she saw only disappointment. As quickly as it had flared up, all the obstinacy drained out of her, leaving her feeling guilty and ashamed of herself. She'd let him down, fallen at the first hurdle.

"I'm sorry," she whispered. Without another word, she lowered her body until her forehead rested on the soft carpet. Stretching her arms behind her back, she assumed the position demanded of her and closed her eyes.

At first, all she was aware of was her own discomfort so, to try to distract herself she listened to the sounds around her. Christina giggled at something Cleo had said, a Dungeon Monitor was explaining to someone how to operate the hoist, the unmistakable sound of a flogger hitting bare flesh teased her senses. Muffled voices, nervous laughter and stifled moans told her she was missing out on the fun and the first seeds of regret set in. Gradually, the sounds faded and all she could hear was the blood rushing to her head, pounding in her ears. And all she could see through her closed eyes was the expression that had been on Jake's face when she'd so rudely snapped at him.

She'd been out of order—after all, he'd only been looking out for her, making sure she didn't put herself in jeopardy by drinking too much. Tears pooled under her eyelids as it dawned on her that this was never going to work. Okay, she might still like to be spanked now and again, but she just wasn't submissive anymore. She couldn't give Jake what he needed and deserved. But if that was the case, why did she feel so gutted about the fact that she'd let him down? And why did being forced to remain in this position somehow calm her down? She wanted to get up, to tell Jake how sorry she was and to make it up to him. She wanted to please him. She wanted to submit to him, damn it.

But the first step in making amends was for her to remain where she was. Jake would allow her up when he was good and ready, and when he did, she would show him how sorry she was.

The sound of movement near her head interrupted her inner turmoil and she opened her eyes to see what it was. Squinting to the side, she could just about make out a pair of heavy, black boots a few inches from her head.

"Has your sub been misbehaving again, Jake?" Marco's deep voice sounded grim, and shame washed over her again.

"Yeah, she seems to be having a problem remembering how to address her Master," replied Jake.

"I believe the stocks are free if you want to punish her some more." Was that a hint of laughter in Marco's voice?

"Hmm, I might just take you up on that. Or maybe I should give her one more chance to redeem herself?"

Jake sounded more like himself now. Had he forgiven her?

Marco chuckled. "Are you still okay if I borrow her for the rope demo?"

Frankie assumed Jake must have nodded because Marco then said, "Great. It'll start in about thirty minutes." The boots then disappeared from her view leaving her heart thundering in her chest. *Oh God, the rope demo.*

"So, Frankie. Are you prepared to show me how sorry you are?" asked Jake.

"Yes, Sir," she mumbled into the carpet, without looking up.

"You may sit up, but remain on your knees."

The order sent a jolt of excitement through her as she guessed what it was he expected her to do in order to redeem herself.

As she raised her head, followed slowly by her body she blinked and adjusted to being upright again. Then she met Jake's gaze and was relieved when she saw the warmth had returned.

"Do you have anything to say to me, Frankie?"

All her thoughts were scrambled in her head. How could she accurately convey how awful she felt for disappointing him like that? She decided to keep it simple. "I'm sorry I was rude to you, Master." She meant it as well. The time on the floor had done its job.

"Good girl. Now suck my cock." It wasn't a request, and Frankie's pulse soared. This she could do, audience or no audience. Jake had trained her well in the early days, stripping her of any inhibitions she'd had and, as long as they were in a safe BDSM environment, she'd soon learned to please her Master in front of other people.

Not taking her eyes off him, she reached out and unzipped him. His cock, already semi-hard, sprang invitingly out and her mouth watered as she watched it grow. Jake was extremely well endowed, larger than any man she'd ever been with. Well, except for Marco, whose cock was the only one that came close. Her lips twitched in a small smile as she remembered servicing both men a long time ago. *Mmm, that has got to be one of the hottest scenes I've ever had.* Jake usually never shared her with anyone, but Marco had been the exception and she had had the privilege of playing with Marco on two separate occasions.

She licked the tip of Jake's cock and dampened as she tasted his maleness. She loved doing this for him, being on her knees as he asserted his dominance over her while she gave him everything she had. A shiver ran through her body even though her blood was heating.

Suddenly, just licking him wasn't enough and she took the head of his cock into her mouth, drawing him in with tight lips. She sucked and massaged him with her tongue, and his cock hardened as if it were steel. Then, without warning, he thrust himself deep into her throat, and excitement soared through her as she opened herself for him. She sucked him in deeper and gagged. Jake withdrew enough to allow her a couple of deep breaths before he plunged back in. Jake loved to see her gag on his cock but he always made sure she was okay.

With every thrust, she took him deeper until she felt his balls brush against her face. Her clitoris ached with need as her arousal intensified, and when Jake's cock thickened, she had to make a huge effort to stop herself from coming. Then, just as she wondered if he were going to come in her mouth or on her face, Jake unexpectedly pulled out, leaving her feeling empty and needy.

"Sir?" Had she done something wrong? She looked up at him and waited for a sign that she should continue.

But Jake took his cock and stuffed it back into his trousers, with difficulty, and gently stroked the top of her head.

"You did well, my love, but we'll finish this later. You've got a date with Marco soon and you need some water first." His eyes creased at the corners letting her know he hadn't forgotten that it had been water that had got her into trouble in the first place.

She smiled. "I promise to drink it and not throw it over you, Master."

Jake laughed and pulled her back up to sit with him. She snuggled happily into him and glanced around. She noticed that the few people who had been watching her suck Jake's cock had already returned to their own activities. She grinned. Only in a BDSM club could she do something so intimate in public and hardly get a second glance.

A squeal from the direction of the St. Andrew's Cross made her look up, just in time to see Cleo drape a light flogger softly over Christina's breasts. Christina was restrained facing away from the cross, leaving her front exposed. She'd been stripped of her dress and her nipples puckered in response to the soft suede fronds of the flogger. Cleo took her right nipple into her mouth and must have given it a bite because Christina's eyes watered as she let out another cry.

Frankie grinned at Jake and whispered, "It looks like Christina has come to the right place."

"We'll see if she has survived when Cleo's finished with her," said Jake, with a chuckle. "I hear she's a very demanding Domme."

"Is Cleo gay?" asked Frankie.

Jake shook his head. "Not that I'm aware of. I think she's bisexual because I'm sure I remember Marco saying something about her being engaged to be married once. To a man," he added, with a grin.

"Christina must be bi as well," mused Frankie. "She and Cleo have certainly hit it off."

Jake nodded and ran his finger up and down her arm with a feathery light touch. Frankie shivered as little goosebumps appeared in response. When Jake put his mouth to her ear and lightly nibbled her lobe, the goosebumps tingled as her skin became more sensitive.

"Thank you," whispered Jake, so softly that she might have missed it if his mouth hadn't been touching her ear.

"What for?"

"For being you." He reached out and turned her head gently to face him.

As she looked into the dark blue depths of his eyes, she wondered how she could ever have doubted that he still loved her. And to think she'd questioned her own feelings for him. Was she mad?

The moment seemed to envelope them in a bubble, stopping time and the existence of everyone except each other. A feeling of calm that she hadn't experienced for a very long time settled over her and she savored it, not wanting it to end.

"Frankie. It's time for the Shibari demonstration. Are you ready?"

Marco's deep voice broke into her contentment and she felt as though the bubble had been burst with a needle. She looked at Jake who smiled and nodded his head. *Oh crap*. Why was she so nervous? She'd done it before.

"Go and kneel by the stage please," said Marco. He held out his hand and helped her up from the sofa.

Without another word she walked as gracefully as she could across the room to the small stage.

Before she lowered herself to her knees, she glanced back at Jake and Marco. They were talking, probably agreeing on what Marco could and couldn't do to her. Her stomach somersaulted as reality dawned on her. Marco was going to strip her in front of the guests. She knew that because he hated his subs wearing clothes when he bound them in rope. Her one consolation was that this was a beginner's demonstration so there was at least a small chance he wouldn't suspend her upside down with her private bits on display to everyone.

Sinking to her knees, Frankie waited. She tried to ignore the anxiety gnawing away in her belly, but there was no escaping the thunderous banging in her chest as her heartbeat accelerated.

No one seemed to take any notice of her kneeling alone by the stage. The spotlights were still dimmed and there was no activity going on around it. But then apprehension started to set in. *Oh God, what am I doing?* She had too much time to speculate about what lay ahead — that was the problem. Then, suddenly, she was blinded by a bright light and she froze — a rabbit caught in a headlight. *I can't do this*. The heat of the spotlight settled on her damp skin, or was it the gaze of curious eyes as people turned to look at the stage? *Why, why, why did I agree to this?* Had she completely lost her mind?

The anxiety she'd felt a moment ago intensified to terror and she closed her eyes to try to shut it out. She seemed to be losing control of her body, leaving her completely paralyzed. What was wrong with her? Why couldn't she move? Why could she only breathe in short, shallow gulps of air? Then she thought she felt something on her shoulder. Was it a hand?

"Frankie. Look at me."

Marco's voice cut through the fog of panic in her head, calming her enough to register what it was he'd said. He wanted her to look at him. *Okay, I can do that.* She sought his eye contact and had to keep raising her eyes for what felt like an eternity before she met his dark gaze.

"What's wrong, petal?" demanded Marco. Although his voice was firm, there was no impatience or anger in it. The couple of times she had scened with him and Jake in the past they'd given her the pet name and now it reassured her further.

"I'm afraid, Sir," she whispered, her voice breaking as she fought back tears.

Marco chuckled. "You? Afraid? Frankie, you've always loved being the subject for rope work, that's why I asked you and not one of the house slaves." He knelt down next to her and stroked her cheek softly with rough fingers. "This was meant to be a gift for you. I wanted to give you something I know you used to love. Remember the feel of the hemp against your naked skin?"

She did remember and trembled at the thought. Marco smiled. "You don't have to do this, you know."

No, she didn't, did she? Somehow she'd forgotten what it actually was that Marco was about to do. He wanted to strip her and bind her tightly in rope. She'd always loved that, so what the hell was wrong with her?

"I think you're more afraid of rediscovering the pleasures of bondage and submission than the actual act itself. Remember, petal, that wanting and enjoying this doesn't stop you from being the strong and successful woman you are. You'd just be acknowledging your sexuality and having a damn good time doing so."

Something in his words rang true. *Yes, that's it*. He was right. Submission didn't make her any less of the woman she'd become. She smiled and nodded at Marco, feeling so much better.

"All right, Sir, I'll do it."

Marco's dark eyes bored into her, as if assessing if she really was okay. Suddenly, the idea that he might decide she wasn't up to it sent a little chill through her.

"Please, Marco. I really want this. Please use me for the demo." Oh God, she really wanted it. She wanted Jake to watch as she lost the freedom to move her body, as she became helpless and desperate for release. And she didn't mean release from the ropes. She looked imploringly into Marco's face, wanting him to see that she was fine. When he smiled, she let out the breath she'd been holding.

"All right." He chuckled then added, "If you're really good Jake might even let you come later." As Marco spoke, he reached out, took a handful of her hair and gave it a tug.

God, how she loved having her hair pulled.

He'd know how his words would have turned her on, so she just grinned demurely back at him and lowered her eyes to show him she had just handed him all of her control.

"I can read your responses quite well, but let me know if anything gets too much. Okay?"

"Yes, Sir."

She glanced across at Jake and saw his worried frown. "*Are you okay?*" he mouthed, silently.

She nodded and smiled. Yeah, she was fine now. She watched the lines, which were furrowing his brow, disappear and be replaced by a look of absolute devotion and pride. That look alone gave her the strength to do anything and she looked up at Marco and smiled. *I'm ready.*

Chapter Seven

"Ladies and Gentlemen."

The room fell silent.

At the sound of Marco's voice everyone turned to face the stage and those who had been brave enough to experiment with some of the equipment stopped. "As part of your introduction tonight I'm going to give you a short and simple Shibari demonstration. Shibari is the art of Japanese rope bondage and..."

As Marco explained the basics of Shibari, Frankie glanced around the room from her vantage point on the raised stage. She couldn't see much because of the bright spotlights, but she could make out a roomful of heads, all watching and listening intently. She was the star attraction and, now that she'd got over her initial fright, she was looking forward to her reunion with the rope in front of these people.

Her attention drifted back to Marco's voice.

"After the demonstration you can have a go for yourselves. The Dungeon Monitors are on hand to help if you need it. I'll leave it up to you if you want to strip your subs, but I only work with naked subjects so I'm going to ask Frankie to remove her dress."

She hesitated as butterflies teased her belly. *Oh God.*

"*Now*, Frankie."

She jumped at the tone in Marco's voice. The gentle, caring man was gone and the big, stern Dom was back in control.

Her dress had a zip that ran all the way from the bust to the hem so in one movement Frankie slowly exposed her body to the crowd. As the dress slid from her body onto the floor appreciative murmurs from the guests were audible. She was stark naked. Although she knew she had a nice body, she was well aware of the little imperfections she hated so much — like the slight swell of her belly and faint stretch marks on her thighs. Drawing her stomach in, she straightened up proudly and waited for Marco to continue.

"Pick your dress up, Frankie."

What? But that would mean bending forwards to reach it on the floor. She knew better than to defy Marco, though, so gritting her teeth she slowly started to bend down until Marco's voice stopped her.

"Turn to face the wall behind me then pick up your dress."

That would mean her arse would be facing the crowd and when she bent forwards all her private bits would be on show. *Fuck.* Trying her very best not to scowl at Marco, she turned her back to the crowd then reached down to pick up her dress. The whistles left her in no doubt that the audience had copped a good look at her nether regions. Although she wasn't the shyest of people, her cheeks burned as she folded her dress and handed it to Marco.

"Thank you," he said, solemnly then handed the dress to a nearby slave who'd been waiting in the shadows.

He picked up a bundle of rope and held it up for the crowd to see. "Hemp," he said, "is my preferred rope. It's made with natural fibers that are slightly rough to the feel." He pulled a length of the rope and ran it across Frankie's body.

Mmm, that feels so good. Because it was slightly abrasive, it tickled her skin and left tiny goosebumps in its wake.

"You can restrain someone in almost any way imaginable, from simply binding their wrists together to creating elaborate works of art. Remember, always check the subject's circulation. If they start to turn blue, cut them free immediately."

Marco continued talking, but Frankie stopped listening as he bound her wrists together behind her back. Once her hands had been tied behind her, Marco held up another length of rope in front of her face, teasing her as he dangled it invitingly. Then he ran the rope over her right nipple, and she closed her eyes as sensation charged through her. Her nipple hardened as the rough friction became a little painful, and she groaned when the pain changed to delicious pleasure. A rush of heat surged between her legs as her body tingled with arousal.

Marco did the same to her other nipple and by the time he'd stopped they were both hard, swollen and so very sensitive. She swayed as he ran his hands lightly over the skin around her areolae, so soft, so sexy. She wasn't sure where his fingers ended and the rope began, but she started to become aware of a tightening around her upper torso. She looked down to see him wrap the rope around her chest and breasts, over and over. The rope squeezed her breasts and pushed them out. Tighter and tighter. Her sore nipples screamed for more attention as Marco bound the rope behind her back in a series of intricate knots. She knew the crowd would be impressed with the cupless rope bra she was now adorned with and smiled at their appreciative murmurs.

Her smile faded, though, when he attached a new piece of rope behind her and left it hanging down over her buttocks. *Oh no, please, not that.* To confirm her suspicions, Marco pulled the rope taut and threaded it through her legs. She groaned knowing what was coming. When he drew it back up at the front, the rope slipped inside the crack of her bottom and rested directly on her clitoris, and she gasped when he pulled it tight. The rough fibers rubbed against her sensitive clit as he linked the rope with another piece and tied a secure knot.

Watching her carefully, Marco tugged on the rope between her legs and she cried out as it mercilessly tormented her. The feeling was exquisite, so delicious that she wanted more, and yet, at the same time, it was almost unbearable. She bent her knees in the hope that it would make the pressure of the rope lessen and heard a deep rumble as she did so. Marco was laughing at her. *Bastard.*

"Such a naughty sub," he said, giving the rope another tug. "Shall we make this more interesting?"

Was he talking to her or the audience? She couldn't tell and didn't care. She was feeling so good now. The tight bindings of the rope felt secure and unyielding yet, at the same time, it lovingly kissed and hugged her body.

When Marco attached a new piece of rope to the one between her legs she grinned until he wound it around her head and through her open mouth. He'd bloody gagged her with the rope. Worse, if she moved her head or tried to talk, the rope between her legs would pull and rub against her already sensitive clit.

Keeping her head still, she closed her eyes as Marco's fingers ran over her body. *Mmm, nice.* Then he embraced her from the front and she surrendered to him completely. Until she heard him cough briefly behind her and her eyes shot open to see who was holding her. But no one held her – the tightness of the rope was playing tricks with her mind.

Through the haze beginning to cloud her brain, she became aware of Marco suddenly appearing in front of her again. She tried to speak, but the only sound that came out was another cry as the rope pulled against her clit again.

Someone was talking. A deep voice. Something about a connection between the rigger and subject. Trust. A phenomenon a bit like subspace called 'rope space'. She heard it all, but her brain couldn't make sense of it. All she was aware of was the rope. And Marco. She opened her eyes again and met his gaze. He was checking she was okay. She didn't have to say anything for him to know that all was well. All was so very perfect. And anyway, he'd gagged her – she couldn't talk even if she wanted to. Well, she could, but that would pull on the rope. *Oh yes, the rope. Mmm.*

"Frankie?"

Oh yeah, that's my name. She opened her eyes again and her vision was blurred. Marco was smiling. *His eyes are so dark...*

"Frankie."

She smiled in response and nodded her head, but unfortunately her action caused the rope to tug heavily again and it grazed against her clit sending sharp bites of pleasure/pain through her entire body. "Argh," she screamed, and the rope tightened even more, to the point where it was almost unbearable. Her body trembled and her legs nearly gave way as the sensations overwhelmed her.

"I'm going to untie you now, okay?"

Nooo. She wanted to plead with him to leave her bound, but she knew it would be pointless so she nodded her understanding, making the rope pull yet again on her poor, abused clit. She was close to coming now. So close.

Marco removed the gag first, easing the pressure between her legs. She missed the friction and almost wished he'd gag her again.

As the tension was gradually loosened around her body, she felt cool air replace the comforting grip of the hemp and when the piece between her legs was removed, she groaned with her loss. Then the rope around her breasts was released, allowing the blood to flow freely again. *Mmm, it feels tingly. Nice.*

Finally her hands were untied and she was, once again, free and able to move. She missed the ruthless embrace, the rough feel of the hemp caressing her as it tightened around her. Now, she felt a bit lost. Cold.

Marco pulled her close to him while he addressed the audience. "So you see, you don't need to be a Master of rope work to create an intense and highly pleasurable experience. A few lengths of your preferred rope and a few knots are all you need. Thank you."

As the audience clapped, Marco scooped her up in his arms and carried her off the stage and back to Jake. Jake was smiling, his eyes full of love as he took her from Marco's arms and pulled her into his own. So warm, so safe. She closed her eyes and savored the closeness. Jake nuzzled her neck and whispered, "You were amazing, my love. And you've got more to look forward to. Marco and I haven't finished with you yet."

* * * *

Watching Frankie surrender to Marco and the rope had been breathtaking and Jake had been filled with overwhelming pride that the beautiful, submissive woman on that stage was his. Now, naked on his lap, she snuggled into him like a contented kitten. He tightened his arms protectively around her. *Mine.*

Frankie shivered, and he rubbed her cooled skin.

"Do you want a blanket?" he asked, kissing the top of her head.

"No thanks. But I wouldn't mind my dress back. I'm the only naked person here," she replied, looking up at him with a slight frown.

"No. I want you naked for the rest of the evening." He ignored her glare and looked around the large room.

The demonstration had broken what little ice had remained and all shyness and awkwardness was well and truly gone. David already had Sinead topless and was trying to bind her breasts in the soft silky rope Marco had made available for the beginners. A Dungeon Monitor was showing him how to tie a secure knot, and Sinead looked like she was thoroughly enjoying herself. He couldn't see Christina anywhere, though.

He watched one of the house slaves approach Marco and kneel silently by his feet. Only when he acknowledged her did she look up. It was a sight of pure submission and it was beautiful. Jake smiled to himself as he imagined Frankie embracing her own submission. She'd already gone way further than he'd dared hope for when he'd first planned this weekend. When Marco had suggested using her for the demo, he'd worried that it might have been too much, too soon. But she was still here and he still had his balls intact.

He looked down at Frankie as she stretched. She was coming back down now and would need a drink soon.

"Wow," she murmured, and sat up a bit straighter. "When did things heat up so nicely?"

Jake chuckled. "After the rope demo. You were amazing, by the way." He planted another kiss on the top of her head.

"Thanks." She paused for a moment. "How did you feel watching Marco do that to me?"

"Very fucking horny," growled Jake, and gave her hair a good-humored tug. "And proud. Proud of you for being brave enough to do it and proud that you're mine."

She didn't answer, but her body seemed to melt more at his words. He wondered if she'd be just as brave when she found out about Marco's other dungeon. The real one.

He gave her a few more minutes to fully recover then gently nudged her and handed her a bottle of water. "Here, drink this. We should have a wander and check out a few of the scenes going on. Some of these newbies certainly seem to be getting the hang of it now."

He helped her off the sofa and reattached the leash he'd removed before the rope demo. Glancing around him, he saw that the bondage chair next to the stage was now occupied. A pretty, petite blonde woman was strapped to it, her legs spread and secured, her arms tied to the cross above the seat.

Jake led Frankie across the room to watch the couple. A large, curvaceous brunette with pendulous breasts was standing in front of the chair, waving a feather duster teasingly in front of her partner. The brunette had a wicked smile on her face as she listened to the blonde's pleas not to use the feathers.

"Please don't. You know how ticklish I am," cried the blonde. The young woman was wearing nothing except for a small thong and it was very apparent that her pleas were exaggerated as her hard nipples and trembling body gave her arousal away.

Jake grinned as the brunette lightly brushed the feathers against the blonde's stomach. Frankie was also very ticklish and he knew what she'd be thinking as tiny goosebumps covered the blonde's skin. He'd tortured Frankie once with a feather tickler very similar to the one the brunette was using. She'd been tied to a St. Andrew's Cross, facing him, restrained and helpless. He'd blindfolded her so she'd had no idea what to expect. When her body had tensed in anticipation of a flogger, he'd mercilessly tickled her until she'd screamed herself hoarse. She'd come so hard afterwards that she hadn't been able to walk.

His attention returned to the two women in front of them. The brunette was smiling as she brushed the feathers against her partner's nipples, making her whimper. How he longed to hear Frankie whimper like that again as she surrendered herself completely to his domination. The need to master her was still as strong as it had been before. He needed to dominate her as much as she needed to submit to him. It was a partnership based on trust and respect, and the desire to meet the other's needs.

These beginners here tonight would soon discover how much deeper BDSM was than just a bit of fooling around with a flogger. Some of them would undoubtedly decide that it wasn't for them, and fair enough. At least they'd had the guts to explore their fantasies. But others, like the two women they were watching now, were about to discover the other side of kink. The side where steel met velvet and came together to create something intense and beautiful that no one else could ever comprehend.

"Argh…" The sound of a pained cry made both he and Frankie turn around. He smiled as he saw that David had now strapped Sinead back onto the spanking bench and was flicking a suede flogger over his wife's exposed arse. Only seconds after the loud slap of suede on flesh, Sinead lifted her bottom up for more. Oh yes, they were another couple who were discovering the joys of this lifestyle. They'd be back — of that he was sure.

Just then, Marco strode past them and gave him a discreet nod. His heart lurched and he tightened his hold on Frankie's leash. This was it. As adrenaline surged through his blood he pulled her close to him and whispered in her ear. Her face paled as his words sank in. Yes, the fun was only just about to start.

Chapter Eight

Frankie felt the blood drain from her face. Had she just heard right? Had Jake just said that he and Marco were taking her down to the real dungeon? What real dungeon? Jake's earlier warning that he and Marco hadn't finished with her yet rang in her ears and her legs almost buckled under her own weight as shock and excitement tore through her body.

She opened her mouth to ask exactly what he'd meant, but was silenced as he firmly said, "You no longer have permission to speak and, just so you're in no doubt, from now on full protocol is to be observed." Jake's tone held that lethal combination of power and danger that had the immediate effect of turning her insides to mush.

She hated protocol, but she loved being made to observe it. How crazy was that?

Without another word, Jake pulled on her leash and led the way toward the door where Marco was waiting, looking just as powerful and dominant as Jake. Bloody hell, what were they going to do to her?

A myriad of emotions swept over her as she was led out of the room. Confusion mixed with excitement. Anticipation laced with anxiety. Fear of the unknown overruled by lust. Her heart hammered harder with each step she took. Her head was telling her to run, but her body refused to listen. Oh God, she didn't want to do this—after all, she wasn't a submissive anymore. Was she? Who was she kidding? Of course she was. Her footsteps quickened without her agreement and her heart continued to pummel her chest.

She'd been so busy worrying about where they were going that she hadn't noticed where they actually had gone until they stopped at a solid, heavy looking wooden door with wrought iron hinges and matching lock.

She watched silently as Marco produced a key from his pocket and unlocked the door. "This way," he said and stood aside for her and Jake to enter. "Be careful. There's a steep staircase just inside the door."

She followed Jake through the doorway with Marco close behind her. It was dark and it took a moment for her eyes to adjust to the change of light. As they did, she noticed the steep stone steps, lit by subtle lights hidden at the side thereby illuminating the staircase just enough to make it safe.

She looked down. The only thing she could see at the bottom of the stairs was a faint light and she swallowed nervously as she gripped the rail and took her first step down toward the ominous glow below.

Thankfully Jake hadn't allowed her to put her high-heeled shoes back on, but even so her feet wobbled on the cold, uneven steps and she descended slowly with Jake close behind her.

At the bottom, she found they were in a long, narrow corridor. The bumpy, cobbled floor felt cold and hard, and the stone walls looked just as unwelcoming—definitely not cladding put up for decorative purposes. The only light came from flickering church-style candles in wrought iron wall sconces. None of this was for show.

"These are the original tunnels and vaults of the house," said Marco, as if reading her mind. His voice echoed through the long corridor, adding to the creepy atmosphere. "There are two dungeons down here. The one we're going to is the largest and was used to punish staff and local workers." Marco turned to face Frankie and lowered his voice. "They used to torture people here, Frankie."

"Oh fuck," she cried, and had to grab hold of Jake's arm to steady herself. What the hell were they going to do to her down here?

"You just spoke without permission. A punishable offense, don't you think, Marco?" Jake's response just made everything worse.

Marco chuckled. "Oh yeah, she'll be punished all right. Follow me."

Marco turned and led them down the corridor, which seemed to stretch on for eternity. Frankie frowned as she followed. She was aware that they were both messing with her mind. BDSM was just as much about psychological mind games as it was about physical play. But acknowledging that didn't change the feeling of dread gnawing away in her stomach. She knew them both well enough to realize that she had good cause to be nervous.

Finally they reached a solid wooden door. Marco opened it and Jake gently nudged Frankie's back to make her enter. The sight that met her eyes took her breath away. *Oh. My. God.* Where the upstairs dungeon had been welcoming and comfortable, this looked like a set from a gothic horror movie. Only it wasn't a film set.

Heavy chains dangled from thick rings deeply set in the ceiling and on the thick stone walls. Wall lamps, giving a dim, red glow, and flickering candles threw eerie shadows across authentic-looking wooden stocks. There was just enough light reflecting off the mirrored wall to their right to see it had every implement of torture imaginable hanging from large iron hooks.

As the initial impact wore off, more familiar items reminded her that this was just a playroom, albeit a scary one. The solid pieces of dungeon furniture were the same as the ones upstairs. Different shaped spanking benches with thick leather straps attached, a solid wooden St. Andrew's Cross and a gynecological-style medical chair were all standard items in any well-equipped dungeon. The back of the room was blocked off by bars and a dark empty space behind them suggested that perhaps it was a prison cell. *Shit, who needs a cage when you have a real life bloody cell?*

Then she cast her gaze to the left and gasped in surprise when she noticed a large, leather sofa occupied by two people. Cleo and Christina. Cleo was holding a naked Christina in her arms and looked like she was comforting her. Even in the dim light, Frankie could make out dark red stripes across Christina's bottom and thighs. Oh God, what had Cleo done? But the look of pure bliss on Christina's face reassured Frankie that whatever Cleo had done had been highly pleasurable. Cleo was obviously just as good with aftercare as she was with a cane, or whatever she'd used on Christina.

"Hello, ladies," said Marco, grinning at the two women on the sofa. "Are we interrupting anything?"

Cleo smiled back and shook her head. "No, we're finished. For now," she added, playfully.

"Maybe they'd like to watch our scene?" suggested Jake to Marco, who smiled at the idea.

"You're welcome to stay and watch, ladies." Marco pushed the door shut and grinned at Jake.

"The more the merrier, don't you think, Frankie?" As he spoke, Jake ran his fingernails down her back. She sighed as a shiver ran through her body—she loved having her back scratched. *Don't stop.*

"Frankie, I asked you a direct question. Answer me."

"Huh? What?" It occurred to her then that Jake had scratched her back to distract her, and she scowled at both his devious tactics and at the loss of his touch.

A hand grabbed her hair and a deep, guttural voice growled in her ear, "Now, that's no way to speak to your Master." Marco towered over her, crowding her space, controlling her.

Her legs trembled as she fought to remain standing. Luckily, Marco placed a strong hand on her shoulder and pushed her down to her knees before they caved in.

The reality of her position became crystal clear. She was on her knees, naked and at the feet of two of the most powerful Doms she had ever known. And they were both going to claim her. Own her. Conquer her. Her breath hitched as her body melted. How could she have thought she wasn't a submissive anymore? She loved this. Wanted it. Needed it.

Through the lightheaded haze spinning around in her head, she remembered she had been asked a question. She needed to answer. *What's the question?*

Lifting her head up and looking at Jake, she spoke quietly, "I'm sorry, Master. I can't remember what you said."

Jake stroked the top of her head and smiled. "Good girl. I'll let you off this time as I know you were preoccupied taking in Marco's incredible dungeon." He took her head in both his hands and held it so she was forced to look at him. "I know you've been fantasizing about submitting to both Marco and me again. Well, petal, are you ready for your fantasies to become reality?"

"Yes, Master." Her voice was barely a whisper – she appeared to have lost the power of speech. The swirling in her head now seemed to have seeped into her blood. Her body was buzzing, alive with the joy of complete surrender. She knew at that moment she would do whatever they demanded, take whatever pain they chose to inflict on her and obey every command. But she also knew that she was safe. They saw her submission as a gift, and she knew they truly appreciated and respected it. Oddly enough, she was the one who was ultimately in control because in her desire to surrender and please them, she herself was getting her own needs met in the most exquisite way possible. And she had her safe word if it got too much.

She was pulled her back to her feet by two pairs of hands and walked to the middle of the room. Marco pulled her arms up and secured her wrists in a set of thick, leather cuffs attached to a chunky chain dangling from the ceiling. At the same time, Jake attached similar cuffs to her ankles, spreading her legs and securing them to hooks embedded in the floor. Before she knew it, she was restrained and unable to break free. Helpless. A wave of nervous excitement shot through her body as she pulled at the restraints to test them. There was no escape.

Jake traced a line around her breasts and smiled. "The marks from the rope are still visible. That's very sexy." He bent his head and re-traced the marks lightly with his tongue. The cool air in the dungeon kissed the damp trail, sending little shivers across her skin.

"Close your eyes." This time it was Marco who spoke and she wasted no time obeying his command. Within moments something soft covered them and she relaxed, glad that she wasn't given any choice in whether she could see what they were about to do to her.

Then she heard both men circling her, their footsteps echoing in the otherwise silent room. She felt as if she were prey being stalked by the leaders of a wolf pack. Which one was going to claim her first? They stopped pacing and she shivered as she pulled on her restraints.

"Remain still, Frankie." That was Marco's voice behind her.

But then they started moving again and she lost track of whose footsteps were whose. Someone touched her softly on her left buttock. Then a finger brushed over her right nipple and it immediately bunched into a hard peak. The footsteps continued and she strained her ears to try to recognize something—anything—that might identify them. Both men wore leather boots and both walked with solid, wide strides. She couldn't tell them apart.

They stopped again and the room was thrown back into silence. Where were they? She waited, but nothing happened. What were they doing? Why weren't they saying anything? The silence seemed to stretch on for an eternity leaving her feeling alone, disorientated and damned needy.

Then, suddenly, a hot mouth took her left nipple and sucked hard. A sharp bolt burned its way from the nipple to deep inside her lower body, and she groaned as it teetered between pleasure and pain. Just as her body began to ache for more, a tongue took her right nipple and sharp teeth gently grazed it, sending shockwaves through to her core. Then it dawned on her. The mouth on her left nipple had still been sucking hard when the mouth on her right had started nibbling. Wow, she had two men worshiping her breasts at the same time. *Mmm, I could get used to this.*

Eventually they both pulled away from her swollen nipples, and she couldn't help arching forward in the hope that they would continue. But they didn't. Instead the silence enveloped her world of darkness leaving her aware of only her body. Her body needed to be touched. Her nipples remained painfully erect and were begging for more attention. Then they got it.

"Ow!"

Someone had taken both nipples between their fingers and squeezed hard. The pressure remained and the burning pain brought tears to her blindfolded eyes. It hurt. She waited for the pressure to ease, but if anything it just got worse. This was as bad as a pair of vicious clover nipple clamps, and Frankie bit her tongue to stop herself making a retort that would undoubtedly get her into trouble.

The pressure continued torturing her nipples, and as the pain numbed and became almost bearable she realized that one of the men must be using his hands as human nipple clamps. Her body was so busy trying to process the agonizing sensations in her nipples that Frankie was taken completely by surprise when heavy straps of leather thudded against the back of her thighs.

She screamed, more from shock than pain, and was immediately rewarded with another heavy slap right across both buttocks. She swayed on the chain, but the fingers holding her nipples retained their ruthless grip causing her movement to send fresh bolts of pain to join the sting on her arse. The blows continued to assault her bottom and legs, the long fronds of the flogger occasionally wrapping around her thigh and delivering a stinging blow to the front.

The fingers squeezing her nipples tightened, sending fresh flames through her body, and still the flogging continued in a merciless rhythm. After twenty lashes she stopped counting and surrendered to the sensations. Then the magic began. The magic that changed the agony to exquisite pleasure. More. She wanted more. The burning ache from her nipples was now entwined with that of the flogger and she felt herself surrender to the sensations as she began to float. The restraints seemed to vanish as her body wrapped itself in the softest velvet, and the blindfold became transparent as she watched sparkling glitter rain down in front of her eyes.

She had no idea how long the flogging carried on for. She didn't care, it wasn't important. All that mattered at that moment was the pain. The beautiful pain that allowed her to experience the unique high she could only get from such divine torture. But, eventually, she became aware that the impacts were lessening. The flogger wasn't thudding quite as heavily against her skin now. Instead it was stroking her. She groaned. *Nooo, don't stop. I need more.*

But, gradually it did stop and her mind reluctantly rejoined her body. Her nipples had numbed under the firm grip of the rough fingers. In fact, it wasn't until the person in front of her let go of one of them that she was cruelly reminded. She screamed as fresh agony tortured the abused nub, but then warm lips closed on it and a hot tongue licked the pain away. As the hurt slowly died, she became aware that her other nipple was still clamped between the ruthless fingers. *Oh no, not again. Please, don't let go.* "Argh..." She cried out as the blood rushed back, then moaned in relief when the mouth gently kissed it better again.

She hung her head, sagging in the chains as her body recovered from the onslaught. Her nipples ached. Her arse and thighs burned. Her pussy throbbed. She needed something inside her, a finger, a cock—anything. She heard movement nearby and felt a soft, cool breeze brush against her damp body as the air around her was disturbed.

Someone was standing right in front of her. *Oh yes!* But instead of fucking her, someone started to loosen her ankle restraints and, when her wrists had been released from the cuffs, she collapsed into strong arms and savored the warmth of them as she was carried across the room.

"We're going to give you a rest for a while, sweetheart."

The voice belonged to Jake. It was him carrying her. She snuggled into him, seeking his warmth. He lowered himself onto the sofa, with her still in his arms and, once seated, he pulled her close and lifted the blindfold off. She blinked as her eyes refocused in the dimly lit room that suddenly seemed so much brighter. A moment later, Marco covered her with a fleecy blanket and handed her a bottle of water.

"Drink this." Marco's deep voice was husky, but still held the commanding tone that was so natural to him.

Frankie glanced around the dungeon expecting to see Cleo and Christina, but they were nowhere in sight. Marco must have seen her puzzled expression and chuckled. "The ladies have gone back upstairs to check on the newbies."

"Oh," she replied. Her voice sounded croaky, which drew her attention to the dry, scratchy feeling in her throat. She drank from the water bottle, grateful when the cool liquid soothed away the furry dryness.

Jake stroked her hair and Frankie sighed in contentment. Then Marco leaned toward her and growled in her ear, "Don't get too comfortable, Frankie. We still haven't finished with you."

Chapter Nine

Frankie sighed as she mentally prepared herself for the next part of the evening. She was horny and very ready for what was to come next. Whilst Jake had held her in his arms, he'd gently massaged her hands, numb from being raised over her head for so long, and it had felt so good. She'd relaxed and luxuriated in his gentle touch.

Marco had gone upstairs to check that all was well with the beginners, leaving her and Jake alone for a while and she'd enjoyed the brief, quiet intimacy. But now Marco was back, and both he and Jake stood in front of her, towering over her, muscles flexed and cocks bulging in their leather trousers. A fresh spark of excitement ignited deep inside her belly as she realized they were probably going to fuck her now. Both of them.

Jake held out his hand and pulled her up from the comfy sofa. As soon as she was standing, Marco replaced the blindfold and her world was once again thrown into darkness. She was then led across the room and bent over a bench, the cool leather sending shivery thrills across the sensitive skin on her stomach as it made contact. The bench was quite short. In fact, it was only just long enough to support her torso, with her bottom protruding over the end.

Every nerve ending in her body tingled with anticipation and a trail of moisture trickled from between her legs as she tried to guess what might happen next. Were they going to fuck her on the bench?

"Stop thinking, Frankie." Jake's voice sounded deeper now, a sure sign that he was as turned on as she was. She imagined how hard his cock must be. *Mmm.*

As her wrists and ankles were secured to the bench by one of the men, the other one rubbed her shoulders and back, gently relaxing her muscles. When the man restraining her seemed satisfied that she couldn't move, he went to stand in front of the bench by her head and began massaging her scalp. The man behind her kneaded his strong fingers down to the base of her spine. The sensations sweeping through her from the double massage went beyond mere pleasure. As her mind and body relaxed, she was filled with such contentment that tears of happiness pricked her eyes.

These men cared for her, wanted her and were making sure she was in the best place possible when they claimed her. And she needed them to claim her. *Now!* Her pussy was throbbing so much it almost hurt and it needed filling. It didn't matter who fucked her, she just wished they'd get on with it. Then, finally, whoever was massaging her back moved to stand at the rear end of the bench. The crinkle of a foil pack told her he was sheathing himself with a condom. Marco? But there was nothing stopping Jake from wearing one just to confuse her.

Then she felt the tip of a large, hard cock rub against her slick opening, spreading her moisture. She tried in vain to arch her back to give him better access. Why wasn't he penetrating her? She needed that cock inside her. The cock moved down and rubbed against her clit and she groaned as the sensation nearly made her come. Then it moved away again, pushing between her labia and hovering again over her opening. *Now, please, fuck me now.*

But instead of fucking her, the person behind her gathered her hair into his hand and twisted it so he had a firm grip. He pulled her head back and at that moment the cock drove into her pulsing pussy, making her scream from the delicious shock. Her scream was immediately muffled as the other cock plunged into her open mouth and her body trembled with the joy of being fucked by two men at the same time.

Neither of the men were gentle with her — she didn't want them to be. As the cock fucking her pussy drove mercilessly into her, her body was pushed forward, forcing her to take the other cock deeper into her throat. She was filled from both ends and the mental image of the two men pounding into her added to the intense pleasure.

It didn't take long for the first tightening of an impending orgasm to grip her and she groaned as she tried to stop herself from coming. She needed permission, but she was effectively gagged by a massive cock. The knowledge thrilled her and the sensation continued building until she knew she couldn't hold off for much longer.

"Mmm mmm…" She tried to form words around the cock, but it was too big and only muffled moans were audible.

Thankfully, they must have realized she was trying to ask for permission to come because she heard a voice—she didn't know, or care, whose it was at that point—say, "You can come now, Frankie."

As her brain processed the words, the cock in her pussy thickened and, when the beginnings of her own orgasm gripped her, the cock in her mouth twitched. A groan from behind her told her he was about to come. *Oh yes.* Then the first waves crashed over her as the cock in her pussy jerked with its release. She felt the warm liquid through the delicate latex of the condom as it continued filling and she rode her own pleasure as the movement behind her eventually slowed.

With her body still shuddering from her powerful orgasm, she felt hot cum hit the back of her throat and fresh waves tore through her as she came again. Her pussy clamped down on the still-hard cock inside her as she swallowed the hot, pulsing liquid filling her mouth and throat.

Finally, the waves subsided and the cocks inside her withdrew, leaving her panting and satiated. A film of perspiration covered her body, and she shivered as she became aware of her surroundings again. Someone was helping her to sit up. She hadn't even noticed them releasing her from the restraints. Once she was sitting upright on the bench with her legs dangling over the side, the blindfold was loosened and she found herself staring at the two men, standing side by side in front of her, looking very pleased with themselves.

"Who...?" she started to ask, but Jake put a finger over her lips to silence her.

"You still don't have permission to talk until I tell you otherwise," he said softly.

Katy Swann

It was then she acknowledged that she'd never know. Neither of them would ever tell her who had pounded her pussy like that and whose cock had filled her mouth as she'd come so hard herself. And it didn't matter.

She smiled her acceptance and closed her eyes as Jake scooped her into his arms. Her body was heavy and limp as he carried her effortlessly across the room, yet her head felt as though it were floating on fluffy white clouds.

The last thing she remembered was Jake telling her that he loved her, his deep voice resonating softly through her head as she fell into a deep and blissful sleep.

Jake looked down at his sleeping wife as he carried her up the grand staircase toward their room. Still naked, except for her collar, she looked completely at peace, something he hadn't seen in a very long time.

He grinned as images of Frankie's flogging flashed before his eyes. Christ, that had been hot. With her naked body stretched and her legs forced apart by the ankle restraints secured to the floor, she had never looked more vulnerable or more beautiful.

He managed to get the door to their room open, stepped inside then carefully nudged the door shut with his foot. He didn't want to wake Frankie, she deserved to sleep now. She needed it. He carried her across to the bed and gently laid her down. Mumbling something in her sleep she rolled onto her side. That gave him a chance to undo her collar without disturbing her. Once he'd gotten the collar off, he turned her over and pulled the duvet from under her before covering her with the soft, feathery down. Then he sat down on a nearby chair and watched her sleep.

He must have remained in that chair for a couple of hours, the calm silence giving him a chance to think and relive some of the evening's events.

When Marco had suggested taking Frankie down to the dungeon he hadn't been sure at first, but when he'd seen her reaction to the rope bondage he'd changed his mind. Frankie liked and trusted Marco and so did he. He knew Marco would never cross any unacceptable lines and would only want what he himself wanted — Frankie's ultimate pleasure.

He smiled to himself as Frankie stretched out, with a soft sigh escaping from her lips. The sound she'd made earlier when she'd tried so hard to ask for permission to come had been his undoing. He grinned to himself and rubbed his cock. Damned if he wasn't getting hard again just thinking about it.

Frankie's needs had certainly been met tonight. As had his. The Dom in him had been hidden beneath the surface for these last two years, waiting to come back out and re-conquer his beautiful wife. But the time had never been right — she hadn't been ready. Until now.

As his cock grew in the tight confines of his leather trousers, he realized it needed taking care of fast. Standing up, he stretched and turned away from Frankie. He wasn't going to bother her now — she needed to save her strength for tomorrow. After closing the door to the bathroom as quietly as possible, he turned on the shower and waited for the water to start steaming before stepping under the powerful flow. Lifting his face upwards, he closed his eyes against the stream and was flooded with erotic images of Frankie.

Ten minutes later, he stepped out of the shower refreshed, with a smile on his face and his cock emptied. At least now he'd be able to get some sleep without the urge to fuck Frankie every five minutes.

But an hour later, he was still awake and growing increasingly restless. For some reason, sleep eluded him. His body was exhausted, but his brain didn't seem to want to switch off. Reminders of Frankie's recent aloofness had crept back in to taunt him and he became increasingly worried that maybe things weren't as right as he'd thought they were. It wasn't anything specific that was bothering him, just a niggling feeling deep in his gut. And it wouldn't go away.

He'd pinned all his hopes on this weekend, but was it enough? Was demanding her submission really going to make everything all right? What if he'd been wrong? What if their problems ran deeper than he'd realized? The possibility that his marriage might not be as secure as he'd thought sent a chill through him that formed a hard rock in the pit of his stomach. He couldn't—wouldn't lose her. The longer he lay and dwelled on it, the more restless and agitated he became until, finally, he decided to get up.

He grabbed a pair of jeans and a T-shirt from his overnight bag and put them on. After a quick check that Frankie was still asleep, he slipped quietly out of the room, pulling the door shut with a soft click.

He made his way downstairs and toward the bar. Marco had told him he was welcome to help himself to a drink anytime and that's what he intended to do. The house was silent, with only a few dimmed recessed ceiling lights breaking the darkness and he was glad of it—he needed the subdued solitude.

He pushed open the heavy oak door to the bar and stepped inside. A lamp had been left on and the soft glow beckoned him inside the large room that looked more like a library than a hotel bar. One wall was lined with floor to ceiling bookcases filled with what looked like original edition hardbacks. The comforting smell of the old books lingered in the air along with a faint smoky tang from a dying fire in the huge stone fireplace. Jake sighed and relaxed as he welcomed the tranquil ambience. The only sound, apart from the occasional crackle from the embers, was the rhythmic ticking of an old grandfather clock that blended subtly into the peaceful atmosphere of the room. This was his idea of heaven.

"Can't sleep?"

The voice broke the calm stillness, making him jump and he swung round toward the bar. He hadn't noticed the dark figure sitting at the end of the bar watching him. He grinned and strode over to join Marco.

"Nah, I've got some shit on my mind. How about you? I seem to remember you always were a bit of a night owl."

Marco chuckled and rose from the stool he'd been sitting on. "I've just finished going through some paperwork. I often enjoy a quiet drink before I go to bed. Join me?" Without waiting for an answer he reached up for an extra glass and poured a generous shot of golden liquid into it.

"Thanks." Jake took the glass and raised it to Marco before taking a sip. The smooth brandy warmed his throat and he relaxed some more.

"How's Frankie?"

Jake smiled. "Sleeping like a baby."

Marco nodded, his expression solemn. "And you?"

Jake shrugged. "Oh, you know."

Marco didn't respond, which Jake was thankful for, and instead they concentrated on catching up on old times, reminiscing about their school days and Marco's stint as a rock star.

"So, why was Frankie under the misguided illusion that she wasn't a submissive anymore?" asked Marco, frowning.

Although Jake had prepared himself for the more personal stuff, Marco's question still unsettled him. He scratched the day old stubble on his chin and thought about his answer. "As her business took off she became increasingly busy and I saw less and less of her. She hardly had time for dinner with me let alone our D/s relationship. As she acquired more employees and became more powerful, I think the idea of submitting felt wrong for her. I tried to explain that a lot of submissives have very important jobs, often controlling large businesses and their employees, but she wouldn't listen." Jake frowned as he recalled Frankie's cold, dismissive tone whenever he'd tried to bring the subject up.

"So it's nothing to do with the baby then?" asked Marco, picking up the brandy bottle and pouring them both another drink.

Jake stared at Marco for a moment, slowly absorbing his words. "Well, no. Of course not," he said, his voice faltering. Frankie never spoke of the miscarriage and certainly had never mentioned it when he'd tried to get her interested in kink again.

Marco raised an eyebrow. "How does she feel about the miscarriage now? Has she come to terms with it?"

Jake was about to say yes, but stopped and thought for a moment. "Well, to be honest, I don't know." Even he could hear the uncertainty in his own voice.

"What do you mean, you don't know?" Marco looked incredulous, and Jake shifted uncomfortably in his seat.

"She won't talk about it. When I bring it up she changes the subject. I haven't pushed her out of respect for her feelings." Jake stared into his glass, swirling the little remaining liquid around it.

"Mate, you've got to talk to her. You owe her that, but don't forget, she also owes you the same. It was your baby too."

Marco's voice was uncharacteristically gentle, which brought a lump to Jake's throat. Marco was right. If they couldn't talk about something so important to both of them, what chance did they have of saving their marriage? Finishing his drink, he resolved that one way or another he would make Frankie open up to him. Even if it meant driving her to distraction with relentless probing. And maybe whilst restrained and helpless? Yes, by the time he was finished with her, she'd be begging to talk to him.

Chapter Ten

The minute Frankie opened her eyes the following morning she closed them again. *Too bright*. With an irritated grunt, she burrowed her head under the duvet and tried to remember how she'd gotten to bed last night. She should be able to remember — she certainly hadn't been drunk as Jake had seriously limited her alcohol consumption.

Her annoyance deepened. Why had she let Jake decide whether she could have a drink or not? She was a grown woman for God's sake. Memories began to trickle back into her waking mind — the rope demo, the flogging, the sex. Who did Jake think he was, making her submit like that? How dare he tell her what to do? And why the hell had he opened the curtains so bloody early?

As one grumpy thought added to another, she groaned when she heard the bathroom door open. He'd bloody better leave her alone this morning or he'd be the one on his fucking knees. On second thoughts, no. The idea of Jake in any kind of submissive position wasn't a good one. She knew plenty of people who were switches, but she wasn't one of them. She was happy with being a submissive. *What? No, no, no, I'm not a fucking submissive. End of.*

"Good morning, sleepyhead."

Jake's bright voice didn't do anything to help her bad mood so she didn't answer and willed him to go away.

"Come on, baby, or we'll miss breakfast." He pulled the duvet down by the top corner, once again exposing her eyes to the bright light.

"Go away." She snatched the duvet back and covered her head again.

"Frankie? What's wrong?"

She hadn't bargained for his genuine concern and she felt awful for being such a misery guts. But, still, if he'd just leave her alone... The edge of the mattress compressed and her heart sank—he wasn't about to give up. With an exasperated sigh, she flung the corner of the duvet down and glared at him.

"Well? What's the matter?" Jake's dark eyes challenged her own and, damn it, she was the first to look away. *He'd better not go all Dom on me again.*

"Nothing," she mumbled and rolled onto the other side of the bed where she could make a quick escape.

"Go and get a shower," said Jake, with a hint of an edge to his voice. "Breakfast finishes in forty-five minutes and you wouldn't want to miss it, would you? I know how much you like a hotel breakfast."

He had a point. Her favorite part of staying in a hotel was the cooked breakfast and she had a feeling that the one here wouldn't disappoint. Slowly, she dragged herself out of the bed and headed toward the bathroom.

"Come on. Scoot." He laughed and slapped her bottom as she passed him.

"Okay, okay," she snapped and threw him a look armed with fiery daggers. Then she stomped into the bathroom, banging the door behind her.

When she emerged about fifteen minutes later she felt a little better. The hot shower had helped to wash away some of her grumpiness, but she still didn't feel like her usual self. Although, she was beginning to wonder if she knew who her usual self actually was.

She dressed in silence while Jake read a newspaper. When she was ready, he looked up and smiled.

"You look lovely," he said softly.

Did she? She was just wearing a pair of jeans and a white cotton blouse, nothing special. Her hair hung loosely over her shoulders and she hadn't put any makeup on. She attempted a smile and mumbled, "Thanks."

Turning away from him she closed her eyes in an attempt to quash the helpless feeling of unhappiness threatening to overcome her. Why did she feel like this? If she were completely honest with herself she'd admit that she had actually enjoyed last night. Jake had done exactly what he knew she'd always loved – taken away her control and bent her to his will. He'd seen to it that her every need had been met. So why did she feel so miserable?

Guilt ate away in her gut at her behavior. Jake had done nothing wrong and yet she couldn't seem to stop the negative thoughts swirling around in her head. She blinked away the tears that were hovering beneath the surface and resolved to be nicer to Jake from then on.

After leaving their room, they followed their noses to the dining room, the delicious smoky aroma of bacon guiding them to the right place. They had been told last night that breakfast would be served in a different room from the main evening restaurant and, as they entered the smaller room, Frankie was glad about that. Where the main restaurant was grand and opulent with large banqueting-style tables creating a formal setting, this room was bright, sunny and relaxed. The tables were smaller, laid simply with a white tablecloth, white porcelain plates and coffee cups. A single white rose in a slim silver vase was the only decoration on each table.

A waiter led them to a table by a window looking out onto the large patio that had stunning views across the extensive grounds. Sheep grazed in a field in the distance reminding her that they were far away from the city. Frankie loved this room and, for the first time since she'd woken, she relaxed as the waiter poured her coffee.

Once she'd had a few sips of the gloriously strong coffee, Frankie felt more human and looked around at the other diners. The dining room was only about half full—several fully laid but unoccupied tables hinted that some of the newbies might still be asleep.

David and Sinead were seated in a corner, hands held across the table and oblivious to anything or anyone except each other. Frankie felt a stab of envy as she watched them. She and Jake had been like that once.

She returned her attention to her own table and tried to think of something to say. Anything that would lift the uneasiness that seemed to be lingering around them. Luckily, Jake broke the silence before she said something banal just for the sake of speaking.

"We've got a bit of free time this morning." He took a sip of his coffee then continued, "This afternoon Marco has arranged for those who wish it to have beauty treatments and massages in the spa."

Frankie raised her eyebrows. "Is it a big spa? You know, with treatment rooms and hot tubs and stuff?"

Jake nodded and grinned. "Yeah, it's pretty impressive. Marco showed me around when I bumped into him at the writing conference. He's organized quad biking for those who prefer something a bit more adventurous than pampering."

Frankie shuddered. The thought of bumbling around on some dodgy bike getting muddy and cold definitely didn't appeal. No, a nice massage and a manicure was far more up her street. But was there a catch?

"No kink?" she asked.

Jake laughed. "No, it's all very civilized and vanilla. Cleo is running a workshop for the submissives before lunch while Marco is doing one for the Doms. To be honest, I don't think they can teach us anything new, so why don't we go for a walk into the village and find a nice pub or coffee shop?"

For the first time that morning, Frankie's smile was genuine. "I'd love that," she said.

"Good." Jake looked pleased and poured them both some more coffee just as the waiter brought their cooked breakfast over.

They ate in relative silence, with only the odd bit of small talk. The awkwardness was still there so Frankie focused all her attention on her two poached eggs and crispy bacon. As she ate, it occurred to her that the weekend had achieved one thing at least. She hadn't thought about work since yesterday, and she wasn't itching to get to her laptop.

"Good morning."

The voice made her look up and her spirits lifted further. Christina had approached their table with a broad smile on her face. She looked radiant, as if she'd spent the night having the best sex of her life. And she probably had.

"Good morning," replied Frankie. "Come and join us." She waved at the waiter hovering nearby.

"Are you sure?" asked Christina, slightly hesitantly. "I don't want to intrude."

"Do you think we'd let you sit on your own?" asked Jake, laughing. Before he had a chance to ask the waiter to set up another place setting, a chair had been pulled up and the chinaware and cutlery laid for an extra person.

"Thank you," said Christina, and sat down on the chair the waiter had pulled out for her. She ordered tea and scrambled eggs then turned back to Frankie and Jake as the waiter walked away. "I'm surprised to see you two down here."

Frankie frowned. "Why?"

Christina rolled her eyes and gave them a cheeky grin. "Duh! After last night, I'd have thought you'd be tied to the bed and fucked senseless all morning."

Jake gave a low chuckle. "It had crossed my mind, but Frankie wouldn't have been very happy if I'd made her miss breakfast. I don't fancy spending the day with someone who resembles an angry tigress that has been starved of its prey."

Christina giggled and shook her head. "Okay, I get it." She heaped three teaspoons of sugar into her tea and stirred before adding a generous amount of milk, until it looked like pale dishwater. She took a sip then grinned at Frankie. "It was awesome watching your scene last night."

Jake laughed and Frankie blushed. In the cold light of day her intimate encounter with Jake and Marco was rather too personal to discuss over breakfast.

Thank goodness Christina and Cleo hadn't stayed to watch the second half.

In an attempt to move the conversation on, she ignored the comment and asked, "So, what did you get up to after you left the dungeon?"

Christina looked up from the toast she was buttering, her eyes shining. "Cleo took me back upstairs and made me kneel by the feet of one of the Dungeon Monitors. I thought she was going to tell him to flog me or something, but she ordered me to suck his cock."

Frankie nearly choked on a mouthful of egg. "And did you?"

"Hell yeah. It was amazing. Loads of people stopped playing and crowded around to watch. I thought I'd have been horrified at having an audience whilst giving a blow job, but it was so sexy." Christina was beaming, although a hint of pink had crept into her cheeks. "He came all over my face. Cleo told me to open my mouth and any cum that went inside I was to swallow. It was shit hot."

Despite her reluctance to discuss such intimate things over breakfast, Frankie couldn't help the flush of arousal that seeped through her body at the thought of Christina servicing the Dungeon Monitor in front of the crowd. She wished she'd been there to see it, but she was probably being fucked by Jake and Marco at the time. Her arousal heated a little more and something stirred between her legs at the thought.

Jake looked at her with a knowing glint in his eyes, and she hurriedly tried to hide the lust that must have shown on her face. Now was definitely not the time.

Thankfully, Jake placed his napkin on the table and stood up. "Well, ladies, I'm going to go for a stroll around the grounds. I'll leave you two to chat. I'm sure you've got plenty to catch up on." He winked at them and started to move away, then stopped and turned back to face Frankie.

"I'll see you back in our room in fifteen minutes. Okay?"

His tone was one that demanded a response so she smiled sweetly and replied, "Yes, okay."

Jake's eyebrows narrowed. "Yes, *what*?" he growled.

Oh, for fuck's sake. "Yes, *Sir*," she hissed and glared at him before he turned away with a satisfied expression.

Christina must have sensed the mutinous way she'd just looked at Jake because her young friend frowned and opened her mouth to speak. Before Christina could say anything, though, Frankie got in first.

"So, did you enjoy your first taste of being dominated last night?" she asked, jovially.

Christina's face lit up, and Frankie was relieved to see she'd been distracted. "Oh, Frankie, it was everything I'd dreamt of and more. I feel as though I've walked through a door that locked behind me once I was on the other side. There's no going back."

Frankie nodded and stared out of the window. She knew what Christina meant — once you had a taste of BDSM, you wanted more. It was enlightening, addictive and exciting all rolled into one. So why did she have such a problem acknowledging it for herself? She dragged her gaze back into the dining room and sighed.

Christina chewed on a bit of toast, looking thoughtful, then continued, "It's like discovering you've been let in on the biggest secret in the universe. Do you know what I mean, Frankie?"

"Yeah, I do. That initial gush of euphoria does calm down after a while, though. It's a bit like falling in love for the first time. In the beginning it consumes you, then it settles and you learn to take it in your stride." Frankie saw a slight shadow of disappointment cross Christina's face so she hurriedly added, "It never gets boring or predictable, though."

Christina giggled. "I'm glad to hear it." She shifted in her seat and winced.

Frankie recognized that sound straight away and grinned. "Sore bum?"

"Hell yeah," groaned Christina. "Who would have thought a woman could hit so hard."

"Did you enjoy it?"

Christina put her knife and fork down and seemed to give her answer some thought. After a few seconds she said, "Yeah, I definitely enjoyed it, but it didn't feel like I thought it would. It hurt way more than it ever did in my fantasies."

"I know, no one tells you that a flogging actually *hurts*," said Frankie, laughing. "You hear about how the impact instantly turns to pleasure, but, in reality, you've actually got to go through the pain first to get to that pleasure. You did get to the pleasure bit, right?"

"Oh God, yeah. But it's hard letting go, you know?"

Frankie smiled. Yes, she did know. "That'll get easier with time."

"Do you know what really surprised me?" asked Christina.

Frankie shook her head and smiled at her friend with affection. She looked like an excited teenager talking about her first trip to a nightclub. Her eyes were wide and bright, her cheeks flushed. She reminded her of herself when she'd first discovered the joys of kink.

"It was discovering how bloody uncomfortable it is being tied to a St. Andrew's Cross. I've dreamed about being put on one of those for years, but it never occurred to me that your arms go so bloody numb. I couldn't feel them for ages afterwards and when I could they really ached."

Frankie laughed. "I know. You just wait until the day a stray hair tickles the end of your nose while your hands are restrained. And talking about being uncomfortable, have you tried a ball gag yet?"

Christina groaned and pulled a face. "Oh God, Cleo made me wear one while I was on the cross. My jaw got cramp after about a minute and the drool... It was gross," she said with an exaggerated look of disgust.

"I bet you gave Cleo a hard time," said Frankie, chuckling as she imagined Christina trying to get the upper hand with Cleo.

"Apparently, I'm what's referred to as a brat," said Christina in mock affront.

"Now, why doesn't that surprise me?" replied Frankie, laughing.

Without being asked, the waiter brought fresh tea and coffee to their table. Frankie knew Jake would be waiting for her upstairs soon and she was about to decline when the waiter offered to pour her a cup. But she was enjoying her chat with Christina and, anyway, she fancied another cup of coffee. *Screw him.* He might boss her about in the bedroom, but they weren't in the bedroom now.

When the waiter had left and their cups were full again, Christina looked at her watch. "Hadn't you better get back to Jake? I don't want you to get in trouble because of me."

Frankie frowned and picked up her coffee cup. *Oh no, there's that damned defiance again.* "I'll go when I'm good and ready."

Christina ignored her tone. "You're so lucky," she said wistfully.

Frankie looked at her in surprise. "What do you mean?"

"Duh," said Christina, rolling her eyes as she always seemed to do. "You're married to a gorgeous man who clearly adores you and what's more, he's your Master. He knows what your needs are and your limits. You don't have to top from the bottom in order for him to know if he's getting it right or not. You can trust him to keep you safe, knowing he'll look after you when you let go and slip into that elusive thing called subspace — which I've yet to experience, by the way."

Christina continued talking, but Frankie had stopped listening. Her young friend was right — she was lucky. Suddenly Jake's request that she meet him back in their room in fifteen minutes didn't seem so outrageous. He'd hardly told her to strip and crawl back to their room on her hands and knees. And on reflection, had he been teasing her when he'd made her call him 'Sir' before he'd left to go back upstairs? Knowing him, he'd have meant it as a gentle reminder of last night rather than an outright order to obey him.

She put her cup back onto the saucer with more force than she'd intended to. "I'm sorry, Christina," she said, interrupting a detailed description of Cleo's pierced nipples. "Do you mind if I leave? I really should get back to Jake."

Christina waved her hand and laughed. "You go, girl. See you later."

Frankie rushed back across the main entrance hall, up the stairs and along the wide corridor leading to their room. She let herself in with her key card and called out. "I'm back."

Jake was sitting on a stylish leather sofa by the window reading a newspaper. He looked up and smiled as she closed the door behind her. Frankie hesitated and remained standing by the door. Suddenly she wasn't sure what to do. Should she go and kneel at his feet? Or just wait until he told her what he wanted her to do? Or maybe she should ignore him completely and get her laptop out? Willful defiance battled with her natural submissiveness, leaving her mute and rooted to the spot.

Jake raised his eyebrows inquiringly. "Are you all right?" he asked, clearly not understanding her dilemma.

"Yeah." She smiled and made her way across the room to join him on the sofa. As she sat down next to him he pulled her into his arms and held her. He stroked her hair—something she loved—then kissed the top of her head. *Mmm, nice.* She relaxed and deduced that he wasn't in Dom mode and just wanted a cuddle.

"You were two minutes late just now. You'll be punished for that tonight." His words hit her like a bolt of thunder. Despite her conflicting emotions about submitting, her body melted a little while her pussy dampened.

A part of her wanted to tell him he was damned lucky she had come back up at all and yet another part wanted her to throw herself at his feet and heartily agree that, yes she should definitely be punished. Not knowing what to say, she decided that it might be best not to say anything.

He pulled away and held her face in his hands, forcing her to look straight at him. His steely gaze was softened by the faint laughter lines framing the corners of his eyes. She couldn't read their expression or his intentions and that both unnerved and excited her.

"Take off your clothes, sweetheart, then kneel for me." He spoke in a soft voice but there was no mistaking the authority he was exerting over her.

This was her moment to stand her ground, to tell him that she wasn't his puppet. So why the hell was her heart hammering so hard in her chest that she could barely breathe? The subtle damp arousal that had stirred between her legs a moment ago now turned into a persistent ache. Not needing to think any more about it, she finally gave up the fight and murmured, "Yes, Master."

Chapter Eleven

As Frankie unbuttoned her blouse exposing the white lacy bra underneath, Jake's cock hardened. *Fuck, she's gorgeous.* He managed to ignore the growing pressure in his trousers and continued to watch her in silence. She took off the blouse then folded it neatly before placing it on the chair next to her. Her beautiful breasts were full and ripe, the nipples already hard underneath the thin material of her bra. He fought to resist the temptation to reach out and bury his face in between the peachy globes and concentrated instead on keeping his demeanor stern and controlled.

Without taking her eyes off him, she undid her jeans and slowly slid them down to the floor. As she stepped out of them, she wobbled trying to keep her balance. His natural instinct was to reach out and help support her, but he kept his hands firmly on his lap, determined to let her do this at her own pace. He loved watching her strip just for him and he knew she loved it when he sat back and scrutinized her, as if he were inspecting his property. She'd once told him that one of her favorite things was being made to strip naked whilst he remained fully dressed. Apparently that sent her beautiful little head into submissive freefall. He fully intended to use that information now.

He hadn't intended for anything kinky or even sexual to happen this morning. But the look of uncertainty on her face as she'd rushed in through the door had practically taken his breath away. She needed his dominance and he wasn't going to disappoint her. He had no idea if she really had been two minutes late or not, he'd made that up just to get a reaction. And he'd gotten exactly the reaction he'd hoped for. Despite all her protestations that she wasn't a submissive anymore she sure as hell acted like one.

His blood heated as she undid the front catch of her bra, exposing her breasts. Her nipples were begging for attention—hard and dark pink, ready to be played with. Now, the only item of clothing left on her was her knickers, which typically of Frankie, matched her bra. She faltered, looking at him for approval, and when he nodded and indicated for her to remove them, she flushed before hooking her fingers under the garment and sliding them down.

Finally she was naked. Jake didn't say anything—he just wanted to take in every little detail of his gorgeous wife's body. No matter how many times he looked at her he never tired of her sexy curves. He also knew that the longer he remained silent and left her standing awkwardly before him, the more aroused she would become. A quick glance at her face told him it was working. Her eyes were wide, pupils dilated and her cheeks glowed. *Very nice.*

"Kneel for me, Frankie," he said, keeping his voice soft.

"Yes, Sir." She fell to her knees, this time more gracefully than she had yesterday. It was amazing how fast it seemed to have come back to her. If only she could let go of that one little thread of resistance he knew was still there. They'd have their talk later. Hopefully they would clear the air for good, but now was not the time for talking.

He rose from the seat and deliberately stood tall in front of her, crowding her space, knowing it would make her feel small. Without a word, he walked around her, inspecting her. Her chest rose and fell quickly, goosebumps shimmied across her bare flesh and her nipples remained at attention. He was in no doubt that if he were to put his hand between her legs, she'd be wet and ready for him.

He returned to stand in front of her, still silent. Her eyes were downcast, hands behind her back, pushing those delicious breasts out for him. Submissive. Beautiful. *Mine*.

"Good girl," he said, noticing the hoarseness of his voice. If she didn't know he was aroused before, she would now. "Go to the bed, lie down on your back, arms stretched over your head and legs spread wide."

"Yes, Sir." She rose, clearly trying to be as graceful as she could, and walked to the bed.

He had been close to ordering her to crawl to the bed on her hands and knees, but he could see that he didn't need to push her any further to get her into the right headspace. She was already there.

When she was in the position that he'd demanded of her, he approached the bed, admiring the way her arousal glistened between her open legs. Her eyes sparkled as she looked at him for approval, and when a flush crept into her cheeks, he knew she'd seen his pleasure.

"Close your eyes," he murmured and waited until they were shut tight. There would be no need for a blindfold, he knew she'd keep her eyes closed for as long as he ordered her to. Her sexual compliance pleased him in the deepest, most primal way possible, just as her feistiness thrilled him outside the bedroom.

A shiver rippled across her body as she most likely tried to anticipate his next move. He knew she'd noticed the selection of toys Marco had very thoughtfully left on the top shelf in the wardrobe. Apart from a couple of very fine handmade suede floggers, the selection included rope, cuffs, nipple clamps and even a vibrator. But there would be no need for them now. All he wanted was to taste her. Then, when she begged for the orgasm he knew she would be desperate for he was going to fuck her hard and deep, leaving her in no doubt who was Master of her body and soul.

A frustrated moan escaped from her lips as he kept her waiting. Her arms were stretched over her head as he'd told her to, but her fists were clenched. Impatient little minx. He considered fetching the rope and tying her to the bed, but decided he couldn't wait that long to claim her. A little teaser wouldn't hurt, though, so grinning to himself he walked to the wardrobe, opened the door then rummaged through some of the toys. She'd be desperate to know what he was going to choose and kept his eyes on her to make sure she wasn't peeping. But her eyes remained tightly shut, although her knuckles were now white. *Good girl.*

After closing the door again, he returned to the bed empty-handed. She tensed as if expecting some form of impact, and he almost regretted not bringing a flogger with him.

"Jake? Sir, please," she begged, the hint of desperation in her voice nearly sending him over the edge.

The blood in his cock pulsed so fiercely it caused him to groan out loud, and in response Frankie whimpered. Jesus, if he didn't release his cock from the tightness of his trousers soon he was going to do himself some serious damage. He quickly undid his belt, unzipped himself then pulled his trousers down. Stepping out of them, he sighed with relief as his cock sought freedom. He stroked the solid shaft, helping the blood to flow more freely again and knew he wouldn't be able to hold off for much longer. Nor could Frankie, judging by her trembling body.

He crawled onto the bed and straddled her chest. He had intended to just kiss her to start with, but the throbbing hard-on between his legs needed some attention fast so he reached out and ran his fingers along her lips. Like a good sub Frankie opened her mouth, inviting him into the warm, wet cavern.

"Mmm..." she moaned as he guided his cock into her mouth.

Fuck! As she closed her lips around his shaft, she massaged him with her tongue, drawing him in farther. *Christ, that feels so fucking good.*

He slid deeper in, filling her mouth until he neared the back of her throat. If he'd been a weaker man he might have spilled his seed from that alone. Holding on to his control, he remained there while Frankie worked her tongue against him until he eventually pulled back, allowing her a few gasps of precious air. Knowing he had control of every part of her, even her breathing, gave him a feeling of power that was intoxicating. But ultimately, it was the knowledge that she trusted him enough to allow him such absolute dominance that fueled his need to protect and care for her.

He eased himself back into the haven of her mouth, his cock tightening and his breath hitching as the pleasure almost became too much. He quickly withdrew again before he reached a point of no return. Frankie opened her eyes at the loss and he frowned at her lack of obedience. She snapped them shut again, but not before he'd seen the worried look in them. When he was sure she couldn't see again, though, he smiled. *Good.* She now thought he was going to punish her which, in turn, would heighten her experience. He had no intention of punishing her of course, but she wouldn't know that.

She remained stretched out and still for him as he slid back toward the foot of the bed. As he passed the apex of her spread legs, he caught the scent of her arousal and the need to taste her became all-consuming. Sliding off the end of the bed, he knelt down so he was eye level with her pussy. With a guttural groan, he launched himself toward the heat that radiated from her and buried his face in her deliciously sweet pussy.

He lapped hungrily at her clit before pushing through her soft, smooth folds. *Oh, yeah!*

Before long, a tremble and a moan alerted him to the fact that Frankie was on the verge of orgasm so he reluctantly pulled away for just enough time to growl, "Don't you dare come."

She whimpered in response, but tensed her body in an attempt to quash the climax. *Good girl.* He wanted her to come while his cock was buried in her beautiful pussy, her inner walls squeezing him as they rode their orgasms together.

He pulled her clit between his lips and sucked hard, forcing it to harden in his mouth. Frankie moaned and lifted her hips. *Oh no you don't.* Jake immediately pulled away in reprimand and firmly smacked her directly on her pussy. She screamed and he only just had time to thrust his tongue back inside before her body started convulsing.

"Oh, oh," she cried as she clamped around his tongue.

His balls nearly exploded with the effort of restraint as he savored her climax, but a niggle of disappointment seated itself in him at the same time. Damn, he'd wanted her to wait until his cock was buried in her. Frustrated, he pulled away, leaving her to recover without his warmth.

"You'll pay for that," he growled, making his displeasure clear.

"I'm sorry, Sir," she cried. "I just couldn't help it. I'm sorry."

Without a word, he stood up and glared down at her. Her eyes were open again, another penalty point against her. She did look sorry, though, and he softened when he saw her genuine remorse. Still, he'd clearly forbidden her to come and she had blatantly disobeyed that order so he would have no choice than to punish her. But not now. Right now, all he wanted was to fuck her hard until she screamed for mercy. But there would be no mercy for her now. If she dared to come again without permission her punishment would have to be severe, though that wasn't what this weekend was supposed to be about. Still, he couldn't allow her another orgasm. She was going to have to relearn some of that self-control she had once mastered so beautifully.

Still towering over her quivering body, he spoke in a low, clear voice, "Frankie, I'm going to fuck you now, but you will not come. Do I make myself clear?"

"Yes, Sir. I'm sorry."

Damn, he'd wanted her to come when he took her. Without another word he drove his cock into her hot, wet pussy and fucked her hard and fast. He knew how much she loved it like this and he regretted that she wouldn't get the mind-blowing orgasm she usually got from rough sex. To make it easier for her not to succumb he focused his mind only on himself and pummeled into her, his balls slapping her tender skin as he did so. He came quickly, but it wasn't the ride he'd been hoping for.

He withdrew soon afterwards and looked down at Frankie, expecting to see her glaring at him in frustration and anger, but instead of being pissed off, she looked mortified.

"I'm sorry, Sir," she whispered again and a tear rolled down her cheek.

His heart melted and he filled with remorse as he took her in his arms and cuddled her. He hadn't wanted to make her feel this bad, that had never been his intention. He continued holding her, allowing her to seek comfort from his warmth and, as she relaxed in his arms, he acknowledged to himself that he was just as much to blame for her coming without permission. He had been too busy indulging his own lust to think about the effect it was having on her. He couldn't possibly expect her to show such a high level of self-control after two years. If they survived this weekend and if she agreed to resume their D/s relationship, they would both need to readjust to the dynamics of the lifestyle. He tightened his hold and prayed that he hadn't just ruined his chances of that ever happening.

* * * *

Frankie glanced up at Jake as they waded through crisp autumn leaves on the way to the local village. Was he still pissed off with her?

The look of bitter disappointment on his face when she'd come without his permission had devastated her. She hadn't meant for it to happen, she really had tried to hold it back, but when he'd slapped her pussy like that she'd been powerless to stop the massive climax that had claimed her.

They'd dressed afterwards in awkward silence and as each second had ticked by, she'd become more convinced that this whole D/s thing would never work.

Jake must have seen her look up at him because he took her hand and squeezed it, offering her some much-needed reassurance. He smiled down at her and her uncertainty lessened a little.

They continued walking in silence. The cool air, tinged with the fragrance of woodland and damp grass, refreshed her and her mind refocused on her predicament. She needed to think clearly, put her feelings into perspective and work out what the hell she was going to do.

Yesterday, she had been convinced that she'd left the whole kink thing behind but, despite herself, she couldn't deny that she had enjoyed last night. There lay the problem. She hadn't wanted to enjoy it. If she was really honest she had hoped that submitting one more time would have confirmed her belief that she was now as vanilla as the ice-cream in their freezer.

Now, though, she was prepared to admit that maybe Jake had been right.

So where did that leave the state of their marriage? One thing she did know for sure was that she still loved Jake and didn't want to lose him. And yet she couldn't break down the barrier that stopped her from reaching out to him and she didn't know what to do about it. Her natural instinct when she'd woken up this morning had been to pack her stuff and go home, but now that she'd had time to think she knew she didn't really want to leave.

She owed it to Jake to stay this weekend. For heaven's sake, their marriage depended on it. But Jake would demand her submission again tonight and she knew she wouldn't be able to resist his dominance. Where would they go from here? Could they ever get back to the intensity of their previous D/s relationship? Did she want to?

Why couldn't she just accept who she was? She hadn't fooled anyone with her earlier denials and yet something stopped her from surrendering and embracing her true sexuality. She needed to submit, but she didn't want to *need* it. She was angry with herself for needing it and angry with Jake for wanting it.

She sighed and kicked at a bundle of leaves that had been swept into a neat pile.

"Are you okay?" asked Jake.

She smiled up at him again and nodded. "Uh-huh."

"The village is only another quarter of a mile or so away. Once we reach the main road we should be there in no time."

"Okay." She didn't mind how long it took actually. She was enjoying the chance to think things through even though her feelings still weren't any clearer.

They reached the village sooner than she'd expected and so she put her thoughts to the back of her mind for the time being. The village was delightful, small enough to be quaint, but just big enough to have a rural buzz to it. Locals chatted, children played and dogs barked excitedly as their owners, wearing green wellington boots and Barbour jackets, walked them to the woods.

After exploring the interesting selection of craft shops and antique dealers they spotted an old fashioned coffee shop opposite a duck pond.

"Are you hungry?" asked Jake as he led her across the cobbled road toward the small, cozy building.

They'd had a late breakfast so she wasn't starving, but the fresh air had certainly stirred up a bit of an appetite. "A bit," she replied and laughed when she saw Jake's eyes light up at the sight of a display of fresh cakes in the bay window.

When they opened the door to the café a rush of warm, coffee-scented air lured them in from the chilly breeze. Inside it was lovely — small, cozy and welcoming. And busy. While Jake was eagerly eyeing up the large selection of cakes, Frankie looked around the bustling café for a free table, but there didn't appear to be any. She was just about to suggest that they might have to come back later, when someone waved from the back of the crowded room.

"Jake, look," she cried and grabbed his arm. "It's David and Sinead." She dragged Jake away from the cakes toward their new friends who were smiling broadly.

"What are you doing here?" asked Frankie, giving Sinead a hug. "I would have thought you'd have been at the workshops."

David gestured for Frankie and Jake to join them then shook his head. "We felt it was more important to talk about last night. We've been married a long time and I wanted to make sure that we're doing the right thing." He took Sinead's hand and squeezed it, then chuckled. "It's the first time I've ever ordered my wife to her knees and expected her to obey me. Before we go any further I need to be sure she's okay with that."

One look at Sinead's flushed face told Frankie that she was more than okay with it.

"Well, you won't want us intruding on your privacy, then," said Frankie, smiling. "We'll wait for a free table."

"Don't be silly," scolded Sinead and gestured for them to sit down. "We've had a long talk and have said pretty much all there is to be said for now. Come on, join us. I could do with another coffee anyway."

After they'd ordered cappuccinos and fresh strawberry tarts, Jake and David quickly got onto the subject of motorbikes. Frankie rolled her eyes and grinned at Sinead. It seemed their men had found common ground.

"So, what happened to you last night?" asked Sinead in a hushed whisper. "You left quite suddenly after that amazing rope demo and I didn't see you again after that."

Frankie flushed as she recalled her hot scene with Jake and Marco.

"Well, Jake and Marco took me down to the *real* dungeon," she confided, lowering her voice so nobody else could hear.

Sinead's eyes widened in surprise, and Frankie giggled.

"Did you...? You know... With both of them?"

Frankie nodded and grinned, enjoying Sinead's mixed expression of shock and awe. "I was strung up in chains so I was completely helpless and flogged long and hard. Then they both fucked me." She shook her head as her own words reverberated in her ears.

Sinead shivered and Frankie couldn't tell for sure if it was from horror or excitement.

"Wow, I don't know if I'd ever be able to cope with such an intense scene. I found last night challenging enough."

"It's amazing how quickly you become used to it," replied Frankie, thoughtfully. "As you get used to the sensations you start to crave more. I used to be such a baby when we first started, even a light spanking had me in tears. Now, the heavier and thuddier the flogger, the better I like it."

"And what about having sex with other people? Is that expected of everyone?" Poor Sinead did look worried.

Frankie laughed. "No, of course not. We're not swingers although some people in the lifestyle enjoy both. Jake has only ever shared me with Marco. Sexually, that is. I've been spanked and flogged by more people than I care to remember, though. But it's up to each individual couple to decide what's right for them. And what might not be right now could be just what you need in a year or two."

"Can I ask you a question, Frankie?" Sinead leaned a little closer to Frankie and lowered her voice to barely a whisper. "What's the hardest part of all this for you? I mean, is it the pain or is it maybe the loss of control?"

Frankie gave the question some thought before answering. "You do have control to an extent because you always have your safe word, but I know what you're asking. For me I think it's obedience. I know I want what Jake demands of me and I've freely given him full control, but there's still a bratty little part of me that can't help defying him sometimes. It's always getting me into trouble."

Sinead laughed. "That happened to me last night. I kept wanting to tell David what to do and when he ordered me to remove my top I actually refused. That's when the Dungeon Monitor explained that I'd never understand true submission unless I learn to surrender my own will. He said I was topping from the bottom." Sinead rolled her eyes and smirked. "That is apparently a punishable offense."

"Yes, I remember learning that lesson very early on," replied Frankie, laughing. "And it's true, the real beauty of submission is letting go completely and trusting your Dom or Master to know exactly how far to push you. It's only after you've obeyed him, against your better judgment sometimes, that you realize he was right all along."

"That takes a lot of trust," mused Sinead, nodding. "That's what all this is about, isn't it? Trust."

"Yeah. It's only when you trust someone unequivocally that you can truly submit to them." Frankie absently stirred her half empty coffee cup. She'd truly submitted to Jake and she trusted him with her life. And yet... She pushed an uncomfortable thought from her mind and smiled at Sinead.

Her friend was staring at David, who was still in deep conversation with Jake about their beloved bikes. Her eyes shone with love and her devotion to her husband was reflected in her face.

"I had to pluck up a lot of courage to tell David about my fantasies," she said after a minute. "It wasn't that I didn't trust him but I was scared to tell him in case he thought I was a pervert." Even though she spoke quietly, Sinead looked around her to make sure no one else was listening.

Frankie laughed, "Well, you are."

Sinead grinned back. "Yeah, all right. But I was scared he wouldn't understand and be disgusted. A bit like Christina's boyfriend, I guess."

"Ex-boyfriend now, I believe," said Frankie.

Sinead looked contemplative and sighed. "Yes, exactly. She came out to him and ultimately lost him."

"Sinead. They weren't married and hadn't even been together very long. They barely knew each other. You can't compare them to your marriage to David."

"I know and I don't. That was never the issue when I came out to David. I knew he loved me and wouldn't judge me. I just didn't want to make him feel like he had to do something he didn't want just to please me."

"That's why communication is just as important as trust." Frankie frowned on hearing her own words. Communication had hardly been hers and Jake's strong point of late.

Sinead reached out and squeezed Frankie's hand. "I needn't have worried, though, he's been fantastic. We're very lucky to have such wonderful husbands and Doms, aren't we?" she said looking thoughtful.

Frankie nodded and picked at her strawberry tart. Sinead had no idea that Frankie's marriage was on the rocks. Or at least it had been until yesterday. Christina had said a similar thing at breakfast that morning. Was she lucky? Yes, she supposed she was, so why did she still have such strong doubts about herself?

For some reason, there was still a dark cloud blocking out the sun and she so desperately wanted to break through it so it could warm her heart again. She just wished she knew how so she could give Jake the love that he deserved.

Chapter Twelve

"I think I'll go down for a swim. Do you want to come?"

Frankie put her Kindle down and looked up at Jake who was sitting on the edge of the bed. She stretched out luxuriously, enjoying the warmth of her thick toweling robe. After the amazing massage she'd had in the spa earlier she was far too chilled out to go for a swim.

"No, thanks. I might have a snooze instead." She smiled and reached up to touch his tussled hair, still damp from his shower. When he'd returned from the quad biking session half an hour earlier, he'd smelled of fresh air, petrol and damp grass. And he'd been covered in mud. He'd been like an excited child as he'd told her all about backfiring engines and hidden ditches, his voice animated and his eyes shining.

Now, though, the Dom was back in charge because he narrowed his eyes and gave her a stern look.

"Okay, but don't you dare go anywhere near your laptop," he warned, his tone deep and serious.

Yesterday's irritation burst back to life as Frankie scowled at Jake. *For fuck's sake.* She hadn't even thought about her bloody laptop. She really had been planning on having a snooze. Jake, seeing her angry glare, must have thought he'd sprung her because he reached out, took her chin in his hands and held her gaze with a look of absolute authority.

"I mean it, Frankie," he growled.

Frankie tried to smother the flash of temper that bubbled under the surface. "Actually, I wasn't going to—"

"Look," interrupted Jake, his voice softening. "We're leaving straight after breakfast tomorrow and will be home by lunchtime. I promise you'll have the whole afternoon to work if that's what you want."

"But—"

"No, Frankie. I mean it. No laptop. Today is Sunday and tomorrow is a bank holiday so nothing's going to happen between now and when we get home, so relax. Anyway, I've asked Jess to keep an eye out for anything that might need your urgent attention. Okay?"

Without giving her a chance to say anything at all, he let go of her chin, gave her a light kiss on the lips then stood back up. "I'll see you in a bit."

As the door shut behind him, Frankie was seriously tempted to throw her Kindle at the door. Had it been a paper book, she would have, but she valued her electronic reader too much to risk breaking it.

She rolled off the bed and paced the room seething in anger. "How fucking *dare* he?" She'd almost forgotten about work until he'd mentioned it just now. A little niggle in the back of her mind reminded her that Jake had good reason to warn her. She had, after all, tried to send him swimming when they'd arrived yesterday so she could finish that report. But still, she really had been intending to have a sleep this time.

She turned toward the drinks cabinet and strode over to pour herself a glass of water. As she unscrewed the bottle she willed herself to calm down. It wouldn't do to spoil the weekend now. She'd wait until they got home tomorrow then she'd give him hell. She took a hefty gulp of the cool water, then banged the glass down on the dresser next to her as anger simmered deep inside her. Although the glass had nearly been empty, water nonetheless splashed out of it and onto the wooden dresser. *Damn.*

She ran into the bathroom, grabbed a hand towel and quickly wiped up the water before it did any damage. It was a beautiful dresser, very old and obviously expensive. And it was where her laptop was. In the second drawer down.

She reached down and touched the handle of the drawer, then jumped guiltily back when she thought she heard a sound outside their room. No, she mustn't open it. But she couldn't tear her eyes away from it. It was as if her laptop was sending out a homing signal, willing her to open the drawer and retrieve it.

Her mind buzzed. Jake had only just left for his swim. He'd be at least half an hour, if not longer. If she could just take a quick look at her emails to make sure there wasn't anything urgent that Jess might have missed. She wouldn't actually respond to any of them, she'd just be looking through them. Surely that wouldn't do any harm, would it?

She touched the handle of the drawer again then snatched it back as if it had burned her in reprimand. She tried again, this time getting as far as actually opening the drawer. She hesitated, letting her hand linger on the brass handle. Jake would be furious if he found out. A surge of defiance finally made her mind up and she quickly reached toward the back where she knew Jake had put it yesterday. Fuck him. Why the hell shouldn't she be able to check her emails?

She carried the laptop over to the desk feeling like a criminal. She would have a very quick look and have it back in the drawer within five minutes. Jake would never know.

But, as soon as she logged on and opened up her emails, she forgot all about Jake as she started scrolling down the long list of new messages. Jess seemed to be managing okay without her but Adrian Lewis was waiting for a response to an email so Frankie sent him a quick note explaining she'd get back to him the following week. A few other emails needed a cursory response, it wouldn't hurt to get them out of the way while she was at it.

A click of the key card in their door barely registered as she wrote a detailed note to Jess.

"Hey, beautiful, I'm back." Jake's voice brought her back to the present with such a shock that she quite literally jumped in her seat. Her automatic reaction was to slam down the lid of the laptop, but the offending machine was still in front of her. In full view of Jake. Her heart sank as his eyes darkened. *Oh shit!*

Disappointment thundered through Jake as he stared in disbelief at Frankie's laptop. He didn't need to ask if she'd been working, one look at her guilt-ridden face made that perfectly obvious. He opened his mouth to speak, but shut it again. There really was nothing to say.

"Jake, I..." she began, but fell silent again. She was clearly just as stuck for words as he was.

The air became thin as he drew in a deep breath to steady himself. Without a word he flung down his swimming bag and stormed into the bathroom, slamming the door behind him. He switched the shower on and turned the temperature dial to hot, then stood and watched as thick steam billowed out of the cubicle, as if it were angry smoke escaping from a burning building.

He'd been a fool to think she'd wanted the same things as him. But he really had believed that he was breaking through some of those icy barriers encasing her heart. He didn't stand a chance now. This was exactly why he hadn't wanted her to have her laptop this weekend. It wasn't because he was some control freak Dom who wanted to rule his sub with an iron fist. He knew that once she got back into work mode any breakthrough he'd made would be shattered as the hard-headed businesswoman took over again.

He sighed. If only she'd given him the benefit of the doubt and done as he'd asked, he would have explained his reasons for him not wanting her to do any work this weekend. But she clearly didn't take him seriously enough to go along with such a simple request. He'd assumed if he'd given her an order as a Dom, her natural submissive side would have instinctively wanted to obey him. How wrong could a man be? Why couldn't she run her business and still be the Frankie he'd fallen in love with? That was all he wanted.

He reached into the cubical and turned the dial down, avoiding the scalding stream as he did so. When the water had cooled a little he stepped in and turned his face up to the flow, allowing it to soothe the aching pressure in his temples.

So now what? Frankie had looked guilty as hell when he'd walked in just now, but it was more than likely that that guilt would quickly be replaced with defiance, even anger. But, damn it, he'd worked so hard to hack away at her hard shell and he had managed to catch a brief glimpse of the real Frankie inside. She was still there and, if he wasn't mistaken, she wanted the same things he did. Maybe there was still hope.

He squeezed a large dollop of shampoo into his hand then massaged it into his hair, the citrus-scented lather lifting his spirits. So, how should he deal with this? If he stormed back into the room and read her the riot act he'd alienate her further, but if he ignored her actions completely, she'd think he wasn't bothered. He needed her to stay tonight, to submit again so he could reach into her soul and pull back the woman he loved so much.

Suddenly he knew what it was he had to do. All was not lost. He'd punish her and the punishment would be severe yet would ultimately take her back into her beautiful world of submission. He knew she couldn't resist a hard flogging, one that would take her so deeply into subspace that her mind floated into an alternative universe. Yes, it would be a punishment with a sweet twist attached. Once he'd banished the aggressive, obstinate Frankie, he'd get her to open up to him so they could finally clear the air.

Feeling back in control again, Jake turned off the tap then toweled himself dry. He decided not to shave — Frankie loved the rough, mean look of his stubble, and he needed all the help he could get tonight.

Wrapping a small towel around his waist, making sure his muscular torso was still damp, he opened the door and strode back into their room. Frankie was sitting on the bed and gave him an uncertain look as he approached her.

He stopped in front of her and deliberately crowding her space, he took her chin in his hand and held her gaze.

"You will be punished tonight," he growled, hoping his tone would do its usual magic. He was pleased to see her eyes widen in response. Hopefully that was a good thing.

He let go of her chin, turned away and walked over to the wardrobe. As he pulled out the black shirt he'd planned on wearing, he heard the bathroom door close quietly, followed by the sound of the shower being turned on. Well, she hadn't torn him to shreds so that was positive.

When he was dressed, he sat down in an armchair and waited for Frankie to come out of the bathroom. He had to play this just right—if he screwed up, he could lose her forever. He'd do what he had to do then it was up to her.

* * * *

Frankie's stomach twisted nervously as she opened the bathroom door and walked back into the bedroom. It flipped when she saw Jake, sitting in a chair looking hard and mean. She'd been completely taken aback when he'd come out of the shower, his still damp body glistening sexily. She'd been expecting an argument and had psyched herself up to give him as good as she got.

But his cool reaction had floored her. She hadn't been expecting that and all the arguments she'd lined up in her head had fallen helplessly away.

And now, here he was—dark, mean and in full control. *Damn him.*

A corset had been laid out on the bed, clearly intended for her to wear. She walked over to it and picked it up. It really was quite beautiful, steel-boned black satin with dark purple ribbons. She toyed with putting it on—if she did, she'd be agreeing to submit again tonight and if she didn't, she'd most likely end up throwing it in his face and ruining the weekend. The choice was hers.

His earlier words, rang in her ears— '*You will be punished tonight.*' Somehow, a small part of her that she'd hidden deep inside wanted this punishment. Needed it. She didn't want to fight with Jake, she wanted to submit to him and, more than anything, she wanted him to punish her. Why, she didn't know, but suddenly it became the most important thing in the world.

Making her mind up, she wrapped the corset around her body, walked over to Jake then turned her back to him.

"Please would you help, Sir?" she asked, quietly.

"Of course." He stood up and took hold of the laces on the corset, pulling them tight bit by bit until her chest lifted and her stomach disappeared. It was a perfect fit and it felt wonderful, hugging her tightly as it gave her a graceful posture.

She then pulled on a very short, flimsy chiffon skater skirt that only just covered her private bits, allowing her a tiny amount of modesty. Once she'd slipped her shoes on she was ready, and waited silently for Jake to make the next move. One of the things she loved about submission was not having to make decisions. It was rather nice not having to think, just do as she was told knowing she was in good hands. Now, especially, it was a huge relief not having to make the next move. She would gladly follow Jake's lead.

After fastening the collar around her neck, Jake took her hand and led her downstairs to the same drawing room as the night before.

The atmosphere was a lot livelier than last night. The buzz of jovial chatter welcomed them along with a glass of champagne from one of the beautiful, naked slave girls.

Frankie glanced up at Jake. "It's quite a different crowd tonight, isn't it?"

"It certainly is. It's amazing what a bit of kink can do to loosen that good old British reserve." He laughed, already looking more relaxed himself.

"Hello, you two," purred someone behind them.

They both turned around and found Cleo smiling warmly at them. Frankie grinned when she spotted a sexy flogger attached to a hook on Cleo's belt. The Domme looked stunning again in a black rubber mini dress and thigh-high rubber boots. Her red hair had been styled so she looked like a nineteen fifties burlesque dancer.

"Hi, Cleo," said Jake before giving her a quick kiss on her cheek. "Where's Marco?"

Cleo grinned. "Teaching Christina a little lesson in obedience. Poor girl, she thought that because I let her get away with her sassiness, she could be cheeky to Marco." She pursed her lips and laughed when she saw Frankie's face. "I think Marco will rather enjoy dealing with our wayward new sub, although I'm not so sure she'll enjoy it quite as much." There was a wicked glint in Cleo's eyes, and Frankie empathized with poor Christina. Marco was notorious for his punishments.

"Hmm, you've just given me an idea," said Jake, giving Frankie an odd look. "Maybe I should enlist Marco's help with one of your punishments tonight, eh, Frankie?"

"No! I mean..." Frankie lowered her voice, not wanting the rest of the guests to hear her plea. "I mean, surely this is between you and me, Sir? Wouldn't you rather punish me yourself?" *God, that was bloody pathetic.* Frankie frowned at her own inept ability to manipulate the situation. She was clearly losing her touch.

Sure enough, when Jake reached out and pulled the ring in her collar, forcing her closer to him, he growled, "I'll decide who gets to punish you, Frankie. Don't you like the idea of being punished by Marco?"

He chuckled, and she could quite easily have murdered him in that moment. He knew full well that, although she found Marco sexy as a Dom, she also feared him where discipline was concerned. Not because she feared for her safety — on the contrary, but because, like Jake, he seemed to know every little secret thing that a sub didn't want him to know. They both seemed to know what the most frustrating or humiliating ordeal they could possibly inflict would be. But where Jake's punishments would be more immediate and straightforward, Marco could be devious and complex. Marco had once restrained a sub to a sex swing, suspended from the ceiling in a dungeon, and had then invited every guest to make her come in any way they chose. The poor girl must have come more than fifteen times and was so exhausted afterwards that she had to be carried out of the room. Her crime? She'd come without permission. No, she would definitely not want Marco to take over her punishment.

"I asked you a question, Frankie?"

She looked up when she heard the sharp edge to Jake's voice and knew just how much she'd disappointed him earlier. This punishment was for real and a shudder of fear rippled through her body in acknowledgment.

"No, Sir," she mumbled. "I wouldn't like to be punished by Marco."

Jake didn't give away what he was thinking, he just nodded at her and grinned at Cleo. "I think we're in for an interesting night again."

Cleo laughed, the husky sound making the people nearby look around. Something about Cleo's laugh made people take notice. It was the same when she spoke, she had that rare quality of sounding authoritative and soft at the same time, and the combination was really very sexy.

"Oh yes, it usually is on the second Vanilla Spice night. This is where we get to sort the men from the boys." She turned her dark gaze onto Frankie then reached up and stroked her cheek. "Or rather, the brats from the true submissives."

Frankie's cheek burned where Cleo's soft finger had lightly brushed it. Her words sent a stark message to the core of her being and she knew that Cleo had seen through her bravado. Thankfully Cleo then excused herself and left them to mingle with the other guests.

"Jake, you wouldn't really —"

"Enough," snapped Jake, looking genuinely pissed off. "Let's get this straight. You're here tonight as my sub. You will address me correctly and I expect you to respect the protocol. I don't appreciate you trying to manipulate me and if you continue to do so, you'll add a third punishment to your growing list. I will punish you as I see fit and if I want to ask Marco to take over, I will. You do not have a say in it." His eyes flashed dangerously as he pulled Frankie even closer by her collar. "You need to decide what you want and stop messing around. You have a choice, Frankie. You either play by the rules or you say your safe word now and we'll leave. What's it to be?"

Bloody hell. Had she really pushed him so hard? The temptation to tell him to go to hell was huge, and yet the passion that had just poured out of him had come straight from the heart. This meant everything to him and that made it mean the same to her. She didn't want to let him down and, more importantly, she didn't want to lose him.

She knew, even if she did use her safe word and they stopped everything, that he wouldn't leave her as long she was prepared to do everything in her power to help save their marriage. But this weekend had reawakened something she'd buried a long time ago and she didn't want it to stop. She had to let go of her constant battle for control so she could fully embrace who she really was.

She didn't want to lose Jake as her husband, but she also didn't want to lose him as her Master. The realization finally hit home. *Stop fighting it.* She was tired of fighting her feelings, suppressing her needs and denying her sexuality. And she so badly wanted the closeness back that she'd previously shared with Jake.

Tonight she would open her heart and try to put into words the turmoil that had been haunting her for the past two years. She would submit to him, happily and willingly, and would take whatever punishment he deemed fit. Then, when he cuddled her afterwards, they would talk, calmly and rationally, and everything would go back to the way it had been before.

Feeling as if a huge weight had been lifted from her, she smiled up at Jake and said, "I'm sorry, Master. I want to stay."

Chapter Thirteen

Jake smiled down at his sub as he popped another prawn into her mouth. Before dinner, Marco had informed the guests that those who wished to could feed their submissive whilst they knelt at their Dom's feet. He'd explained that the experience could be highly pleasurable for both involved and often helped put a sub into the right headspace.

Jake had almost taken Frankie over to the tables that had been laid normally but, on a sudden impulse, had instead led her to a table where every second chair had been replaced with a cushion on the floor. He'd been astounded at her lack of objection when he'd ordered her to kneel on the plump cushion next to the seat he'd chosen.

There was no seating plan tonight, the guests were free to sit where they wanted and he'd been curious to see who would join them at their table. He had been delighted when David had brought Sinead across to the same table and ordered her to her knees. She had looked utterly shocked at first, but had soon composed herself and done as she'd been told.

Frankie, who was already perched on her knees, had smiled sweetly at Sinead and had looked pleased to see her new friend. Jake had ordered the garlic prawns to start, Frankie's favorite, and now enjoyed watching her accept his offering with surprising humility.

He exchanged a few pleasantries with David and an older Domme who had brought her male sub to kneel at their table, but otherwise they ate relatively quietly, focusing more on feeding their subs than making trivial conversation.

Frankie looked beautiful as she gazed up at him, waiting for his cue that she was to open her mouth again. Submission suited her. It gave her a glow that left her cheeks flushed and her eyes sparkling. His collar looked so right around her neck and she wore it with grace and dignity just like she had the very first time he'd put it on her.

Right now, at this very moment, nobody would ever know about her inner conflict if they were to observe her eating from her Master's hand. But he knew it was still there and he wanted nothing more than to banish the emotional turmoil that was wreaking havoc with her heart, and make her world perfect again. And he would. The punishment he'd planned for her tonight would take her to the very edge of her limits and beyond. When she finally let go and tumbled over the cliff he'd be there to catch her and make everything all right again. There would be no need for the second punishment if all went to plan.

He reached down and stroked the top of her head, his heart filling with such tenderness that it momentarily took his breath away. She raised her eyes to his and smiled. The look of submissive devotion radiated from her and his need to protect her intensified in response.

He continued to feed her for the remainder of the meal. Time somehow felt as if it had been suspended with them being the only people in the entire universe. Finally, when the meal was over, she rested her head on his lap and sighed contentedly as he ran his fingers through her hair.

Marco would be planning more after-dinner entertainment soon, but when that was over, Jake would take Frankie down to the dungeon for her punishment. The blood in his veins chilled as apprehension brought sudden doubt to his mind. Was he doing the right thing? Was she strong enough to cope with what he had planned for her? His jittery nerves calmed slightly as he acknowledged to himself that, yes, Frankie could take it. She'd be fine. He'd taken her that deeply into subspace before and she had described it afterwards as the most profoundly spiritual experience of her life. That was what he was going to aim for tonight.

Frankie looked up as Marco strode into the restaurant with a very contrite looking Christina in tow. Frankie was still sitting on the cushion by Jake's feet, but had thankfully been allowed to take the weight off her knees so she could sit more comfortably.

Christina was naked except for a thick leather collar around her neck with a leash attached, which Marco held firmly in his hand. Her hands were cuffed behind her back and she looked a pretty picture as she blushed when the guests all turned to look at them.

"I trust you all enjoyed dinner?" Marco's deep voice boomed across the lingering murmurs of his guests.

Gradually the room fell silent until Marco had everybody's undivided attention. "The after-dinner entertainment tonight will be a little different from what I had planned. Christina here has kindly volunteered to be my victim as part of her punishment. She's been a very naughty girl. Haven't you, sub?"

Christina's cheeks flared as every eye in the room was on her. "Yes, Sir."

"Tell our guests why you're being punished tonight." Marco's eyes, although remaining stern, glinted with humor as Christina struggled with her humiliation.

"I was disrespectful and rude, Sir." Christina's face was now flame red, and Frankie felt a pang of sympathy for her friend, although she was quietly thankful that it wasn't her in the spotlight. For once.

"What was it you called me?" growled Marco, loudly enough for everyone to hear.

"I… I called you a sadistic oaf who should go get a haircut," muttered Christina.

The guests snickered, and Marco's eyes crinkled as he tried to keep his expression serious. He pulled on the leash, forcing Christina's face to be eye level with his crotch, and held her there. Grinning, he looked around at his guests.

"Do you agree that this little brat needs to be taught a lesson?"

Everyone in the room laughed and agreed that she should indeed be put in her place. They had suddenly turned from being refined dinner guests to hungry circus spectators. It seemed that Frankie wasn't the only one who knew of Marco's reputation when it came to punishments.

Marco nodded then laughed at something Christina muttered under her breath. Without another word he unclipped her wrist cuffs, took her hand and led her to a table in the middle of the room. The place settings had been cleared and the surrounding tables moved leaving a large space around the lone table. Marco took Christina's head and cradled it in his huge, strong hands making it clear that he had her exactly where he wanted her. He looked down into her eyes, his dark gaze boring into hers, and Frankie knew exactly what Christina would be feeling at that moment. Marco had the power to reduce a sub to a pile of rubble using only 'that' look, and Frankie couldn't help being ever so slightly envious of Christina for being on the receiving end of it.

Marco let go of Christina's head and nodded at the table. Christina seemed to have no problem understanding the gesture and quickly climbed up onto it. She knelt in the middle, legs apart and fingers entwined behind her head. Marco had obviously started to train her already. Still not saying anything, Marco then picked up a riding crop that had been placed on a nearby chair. He held it up for all to see then swung it playfully through the air. The *whoosh* made Frankie's skin tingle, but poor Christina actually jumped at the scary sound.

"Remain still, sub," demanded Marco, then he firmly patted the insides of Christina's thighs until her legs were spread as wide as they could go.

Her eyes watered, but there was no denying the glisten from between her legs. Then Marco placed the riding crop between her teeth and told her to hold onto it.

"If you drop the crop at any time during your punishment I'll whip your pussy with it."

Frankie knew Marco was serious, she'd seen him do it before to a woman at a play party they'd attended. The poor sub had first screamed before being overthrown by a massive orgasm. She'd then been punished again for coming without permission. She couldn't have won, and that was what Marco was so damned good at.

Christina bit hard into the leather and looked as though she might cry at any moment. But Frankie was aware that any tears would be a sign of humiliation rather than real fear. Christina could call her safe word at any time and Marco would stop immediately.

Suddenly everyone in the room gasped as Marco picked up a single tail whip from the chair and flicked it through the air. A loud crack made some people jump, including Frankie, as the speed of the whip broke the sound barrier. Poor Christina looked terrified and Frankie worried that she might actually drop the crop before he'd even gotten started.

"Tonight I'm going to tell you about another aspect of BDSM that you might be interested in." He addressed the guests clearly and loudly, demanding his audience's full attention. "I'm not telling you because I want you to go out and try it, but because it's imperative that you understand the risks involved if you do one day decide to take your play to another level. Edge play is anything that involves risk. Different people have different ideas on what is and what isn't edge play, but the sort of thing I'm talking about is breath play, fire play, blood play. I don't need to go on, do I?"

The crowd all shook their heads and murmured their agreement.

"The consensual element still applies, but where there's a raised risk of injury, or even death, we tend to refer to RACK. Risk Aware Consensual Kink. Note the word consensual is still present. Remember, if it's not consensual, it's not BDSM. I'm not here to tell you what or what not to do, but I do want to advise you to wait with edge play until you have the experience and knowledge to play safely. The safety of your sub is always your main priority. If and when you do decide to take things further, do your homework."

He suddenly threw the tail of the whip into the air again and drew a collective gasp from the crowd as it snapped loudly in the silent room.

"That brings me onto the subject of whips," he continued. "Some people consider them edge play, some don't. I personally do because they can be dangerous in inexperienced hands." He drew the whip up and spun it in the air before throwing it forwards to create another terrifying crack. "This beauty is a signal whip and I'd recommend that you start with this as it's easier to handle than, say, a bullwhip."

As Marco spoke about the techniques of using the whip, Frankie watched Christina closely. The crop wobbled slightly in her mouth as she listened to Marco's warnings about the risks and her eyes were wide and watery. Marco had been a Master of the single tail for many years and knew how to deliver a delicious and safe lash from it, but Christina might not have felt so confident about his skills at that moment.

Marco stopped talking and the tension in the room intensified. He approached Christina and softly stroked her back. When he whispered something in her ear, she smiled shakily and nodded her head.

Stepping back, Marco looked around him to check his range was clear. Then, without warning, he raised his arm and threw the tail of the whip through the air. Christina screamed through the crop and squeezed her eyes shut as the tip of the whip kissed her back, but Frankie understood that the scream was only from fear. Marco had done something similar to her once and, although it had hurt, it wasn't anywhere near as bad as she had first imagined. Marco had used a technique that was both safe and pleasurable. Well, at least it had been once she'd gotten over her initial terror. The experience had turned out to be both intense and beautiful, sending her mind soaring with each stroke of the lash.

Marco continued to whip Christina's back, aiming mainly for the upper half. Every now and again, though, he would surprise her with a lash across her bottom and her subsequent squeal almost made her let go of the crop. Marco was so confident that he even joked with the guests in between the lashes, leaving Christina completely clueless as to when the next lash would hit.

Frankie was just admiring Christina's self-discipline in keeping the crop securely between her teeth when Marco threw a lash aimed right at the backs of her thighs. The poor girl screamed in shock and the crop fell from her mouth. Marco grinned. That must have been exactly what he'd been expecting to happen.

"Oh dear," he said, putting the whip down and striding over to Christina. He put his arm around her trembling body and held her. She'd be thinking right now that Marco was going to let her get away with letting the crop fall from her mouth. Frankie knew different. Marco was as notorious with mind games as he was with punishments.

Christina visibly relaxed into his arms, but stiffened again when he announced, "Now I'm going to have to whip your pretty little pussy."

Christina's face was a picture. The look of horror almost masked the flush of arousal that tinted her cheeks. Frankie guessed that Christina would probably have been floating in and out of subspace during the whipping so she'd most likely be in a highly aroused state. And now he was going to carry out the punishment for dropping the crop. Although the bite of the crop hurt like hell, especially on such a sensitive part of the body, Frankie had a feeling that Christina was about to find out what subspace was truly about. *Lucky girl.*

Marco told her to lie down on the table, pull her knees up to her chest and spread her legs wide. As Frankie watched Christina comply, Jake tugged gently on her hair, forcing her to look up at him. "You're next," he whispered in a dark voice. His eyes flashed with excitement, probably from watching the whipping. But still, the look he gave her sent a shiver through her and she wondered what was going through his kinky mind.

"Hold onto your knees and keep your legs spread," ordered Marco. He had picked the crop up and flicked it playfully through the air, making sure the *whoosh* was clearly audible to Christina. "You'll get ten strokes, but if you close your legs we start again from the beginning. Do you understand?"

"Yes, Sir," cried Christina, her face now ashen.

The first stroke was clearly not that hard, although Christina's body jerked in response. The second stroke was harder judging by the crack of the slapper hitting her delicate flesh. Christina screamed and pulled her legs together, hugging her knees tightly.

"Back in position," barked Marco. "We'll start from scratch."

"No, please, Sir," whimpered Christina, still not letting go of her knees.

Marco waited a second, and when Christina still made no sign of moving back into position Marco asked, "Do you want to use your safe word, Christina?" There was no anger or impatience in his voice, just concern.

For a moment there Frankie thought Christina was going to say 'yes'. The word was formed on her lips, but never came out. She was clearly wrestling with her emotions knowing that if she used her safe word that would be the end of the scene. If she chose to continue, Frankie sincerely hoped that Christina would let go and embrace the pain because only then could she reap the rewards that came with it.

Frankie grinned when Christina said clearly, "I want to continue, Sir."

"Good girl." Marco bent down and kissed Christina on the mouth. When he straightened, he picked up the crop and waited for her to resume her position.

As the whipping started again it was clear that Marco didn't hit Christina all that hard at all, just enough that she would feel a sting. She watched from her vantage point where she had a close and direct view of the action. Although it was difficult to see exactly where the crop landed, she had a pretty good idea of what Marco was up to and her heart rate accelerated in response. He would hit Christina everywhere but directly on her clit. Sometimes the crop would fall on her mound, sometimes farther back on her labia and sometimes on her inner thigh. Each time Christina would groan, but she held her position and took the punishment well.

After the eighth stroke, Frankie's own pussy began to throb painfully. Number nine, she guessed, would be the hardest yet, although she couldn't tell where it would land, and number ten... Well, number ten would surely be the one to take her over the edge.

When Jake had whipped Frankie's pussy once he'd made her start from scratch after seven of the twelve strokes she was to receive. By the time they'd finally reached the twelfth stroke her whole pussy had felt like it had been whipped with fire. Jake had delivered number twelve directly on her clit and the pain had wrung the biggest orgasm she'd had in years out of her. Oh yes, Christina was in for a treat if she guessed correctly.

She held her breath on Christina's behalf and almost felt the impact of number nine between her own legs. She moaned as the throbbing became more insistent and wondered briefly if Jake would notice if she touched herself. Of course he bloody would. If he caught her pleasuring herself he'd probably make her masturbate in front of all the fucking guests. That was enough to ease the urge somewhat.

Christina's wail echoed through the room as she struggled to remain in position and Marco waited patiently for her to quieten down again. Finally, when she appeared to have composed herself, Marco said, "This last one will be the hardest, Christina. You may come if you want to."

Christina laughed cynically, as if the idea of having an orgasm while her pussy was being whipped was ludicrous. The laugh died on her lips when number ten did indeed fall directly on her clit with a resounding slap.

"Oh, oh, oh..." Christina's body bucked as an orgasm washed over her. Tears rolled down her cheeks as she arched her body upwards. Marco moved quickly to stand between her legs, then bent down and licked her pussy, making her scream again when a second orgasm claimed her. She seemed to revel in the aftermath for a very long time, shaking in Marco's arms as he held her tightly.

Frankie looked up at Jake and smiled. Jake smiled back, probably remembering their own scene, but the smile was soon replaced with something else. A hint of the dark excitement she'd glimpsed just before resurfaced and sent icy daggers of fear into Frankie's heart. *Oh crap.* What the hell was he planning on doing to her?

Chapter Fourteen

"Did you enjoy watching that?" Jake already knew the answer. Frankie's cheeks were flushed and her pupils dilated. *Yes, she's turned on all right.* He wanted to hear her say it out loud though. It was important that she voiced every thought in her head so she would find it easier later when he would force them from her. Maybe 'force' was a bit strong. He'd never force her to do anything against her will, but he was going to push her into an altered state so she would have no choice but to be completely honest with him.

Frankie nodded, her lips sensuously parted. The scene had clearly had a strong effect on her. That would make it easier for him to break through to her later. For now, though, she needed reminding of her place.

"I asked you a direct question, Frankie," he growled, making sure his face showed that he required her to observe protocol.

"Sorry, Master," she replied huskily. "Yes, Sir, I did enjoy that. It reminded me of…" She blushed and looked down.

He gently put his finger under her chin and lifted her face back up toward him. "What did it remind you of, my love?"

"The time you did the same to me, Master. How much it stung at first, but then the exquisite pleasure that followed." She blinked and lowered her eyes again. "It also reminded me of a time when Marco used a similar whip on me."

"Hmm. Did you enjoy that whipping?" he asked, recalling the night Marco had expertly whipped her gorgeous arse.

Frankie's eyes got a little wider and her blush deepened. "Yes, Master."

Of course he knew she'd enjoyed it, but he wanted to make sure her memory of it was still a positive one.

"I'm going to ask Marco to give me a few pointers in using a single tail whip next time we're here. I'm thinking of buying one so I can whip you myself. Would you like that?"

"Er... I think so, Master," whispered Frankie, not looking at all sure.

His blood heated at the thought of whipping her creamy white skin, painting red stripes across her perfect body and marking her as his. Not permanently of course, but he knew how much she enjoyed inspecting her marks the day after a scene, and what better marks than the stripes of a whip? He wanted to do it properly, though, and wasn't going to try it on her until he was completely sure he wouldn't harm her, so he'd leave that to another time.

Tonight he would use something he was a master with. The flogger. And not just any old flogger. Before Frankie had withdrawn from him, he'd bought a handmade beauty at a fetish fair. Frankie had been excited and keen to try it until he had given her the first few lashes, and from then on it had become her most dreaded flogger. The fronds were a combination of thick leather strands mixed with plaited rope, with little knots at the ends. According to Frankie it hurt like hell and he hadn't used it on her again. Until tonight. It was pure luck that it was still in his toy bag after such a long time. Well, lucky for him. Not so lucky for Frankie.

"I'm going to push your limits tonight, Frankie." He spoke with deliberate firmness, not wanting to give her a chance to protest. "Your punishment won't be erotic in any way, it will be severe and intense." He was pleased to see a shiver run through her at his words. Was it from apprehension? Or maybe fear? *Good.* He wanted to play with her mind a little to get her into the right mood.

"Yes, Master," she replied, her voice shaking a little.

He bent forward and kissed the top of her head, taking a deep breath as he did so. He savored the familiar scent of her shampoo and delicate perfume. *Mmm, she smells wonderful. She smells of Frankie.* His resolve to succeed tonight strengthened as he inhaled again and tugged gently on her collar.

"Come on, let's go. Marco has given us exclusive use of the dungeon. It's time for your punishment."

Her breath hitched and her body shuddered as she rose slowly to her feet. He allowed her time for the blood to start circulating through her legs again then strode toward the door, knowing she'd be following close behind. He walked briskly along the corridor, toward the heavy oak door leading down to the dungeon. As they approached it, something that felt oddly like apprehension stirred deep inside him. He shrugged the feeling off as he reached into his pocket to retrieve the key Marco had given him. He needed to be strong for Frankie, confident and masterful, certainly not showing any signs of weakness.

As he unlocked the door, he reinforced his control by giving her a stern, unyielding glare then lightly nudged her to make her walk through. They made their way silently down the stone steps toward the flickering glow in the otherwise dark tunnel beneath them. When they reached the main dungeon, he pushed the door open and turned to Frankie.

"After you," he said, quietly. "Go to the middle of the room, strip then kneel on the floor, arms behind your back." He paused for a split second then added, "Then close your eyes and open your mouth."

As he suspected, a pink glow graced her cheeks and a sexy, hopeful grin lit her face.

"Yes, Sir," she breathed, not quite managing to hide her surprise at this clearly unexpected order.

She'd probably think that he was going to go easy on her and that he was going to give her a treat, but she'd be wrong. This was part of his plan to get her into the most submissive headspace possible before the punishment even began. Yes, she was going to worship his cock and in doing so she'd become highly aroused. But he wouldn't give her the ultimate prize, at least not until much later. He was going to leave her desperate, turned on and very needy.

His cock twitched as she undressed and got into position. Once on her knees, she placed her hands behind her back thereby pushing those lush breasts out for him. After a quick glance at him, she closed her eyes and opened her mouth, tilting her head upwards in readiness for him. *Fuck she looks hot.* He stood still and just watched her for a few seconds. He was quickly hardening in response to the sight in front of him.

His cock began to feel uncomfortably tight in the heat of his leather trousers so he unzipped himself and pulled it out. He rubbed it roughly, relieved to feel the blood flow freely again. It hardened as if it were steel as he imagined shoving it inside Frankie's open mouth, her tongue working its glorious magic as he fucked her face.

With a groan, he strode over, stopping just in front of her. Her mouth glistened welcomingly at him, the lashes on her closed eyes fluttering, telling him she was ready for him. Without a word, he plunged his cock into her mouth and sighed with pleasure as Frankie drew him in and sucked hard.

"Fuck," he growled and pushed his shaft farther into her mouth until it touched the back of her throat.

For him, this was the epitome of a D/s dynamic. With him as the powerful Master and her on her knees with her mouth stuffed with his cock. She gave him everything in that moment—her body, her devotion, her surrender and, most importantly, her trust. The adrenaline rush he got from that control ignited every nerve ending in his body and set off sparks of electricity that surged straight to his cock.

"Open your eyes and look at me, Frankie," he growled. He had a message for her and she needed to see it in his face to make sure she received it loud and clear. The fire in his groin flared as she opened her eyes and raised them to meet his, his cock still buried deep in her mouth. *Damn, she's hot.*

"You do not have permission to come. Don't let me down this time. Do you understand?"

A flash of emotion flickered across her face but he couldn't quite work out whether it was defiance, guilt or possibly frustration. Or maybe it was acceptance? She nodded her head as best she could, her eyes confirming her compliance, and returned her focus to her task. Still keeping her eyes on him, she relaxed her throat muscles and took the full length of him into her mouth and throat. When his balls touched the delicate skin on her face, the exquisite pleasure deepened and when he pulled out to allow her some air, she greedily sucked him back in.

As the pressure built, Jake gripped Frankie by the hair and held her head as he used her for his pleasure. She'd be horny as hell now, desperate to come, but he wasn't going to give her permission. She'd better not disappoint him this time. He was planning on leaving her feeling used and aroused so she would be compliant and eager to please during her punishment. When he finally let her come later she was going to be wound up so fucking tight that she'd lift the roof with her screams.

That final thought made his balls tighten unbearably as his body sought its climax. He groaned as the pressure released and sent his seed soaring down Frankie's throat. He kept his cock in her mouth as it continued to spurt his cum inside until, finally, the flow slowed and the insistent throbbing subsided. She kept him inside her like the good sub he'd trained her to be in the early days, and when he eventually pulled out, she dutifully licked him clean.

"Good girl," he said, softly just as the door opened.

Marco popped his head round and grinned. "Sorry, mate, am I interrupting?"

Jake looked down at Frankie's red face. As she was on her knees at his feet, her mouth just inches from his cock, it was blatantly obvious what she'd just been doing. Feeling devious, he grinned back at his friend.

"No, we're done. Would you like my sub to suck your cock too?" He smiled at Frankie's shocked gasp.

But he knew she wouldn't really be shocked—she'd probably love to give Marco a blow job.

Marco shook his head and entered the dungeon. "Thank you for the offer, but Christina has only just finished thanking me for her punishment. Another time, though," he added, with a smile aimed at Frankie.

Frankie blushed and looked down, wisely remaining silent.

"Frankie has been very naughty and is about to be taught a lesson," he said to Marco. "Would you care to watch?"

Marco shook his head in regret. "I'd love to, old friend, but I'm needed upstairs. I've just popped down for a couple of floggers. I'll try to look in on you later, though. Knowing how naughty your sub can be this could be a long session." Marco laughed and strode over to a cabinet where he selected a couple of soft suede floggers. He gave Jake a quick nod then left, leaving him alone with Frankie again.

She was still on her knees in front of him so he ruffled her hair then bent down and whispered softly in her ear, "Are you ready to take your punishment?"

"Yes, Master," she whispered, her voice trembling.

"Use your safe word if it gets too much. Although this is a punishment, I don't want you to suffer more than you can take. Okay?"

"Yes, Master."

Tears filled in her eyes as she seemed to struggle to take in what he'd just said and his heart went out to her. For him to remind her to use her safe word she must be realizing that he wasn't going to go easy on her. He came close to relenting and had to mentally shake himself out of his hesitance. He wouldn't be doing this if he didn't think she genuinely needed it.

She'd once told him after a particularly harsh punishment that she had felt as if the weight of the world had been lifted from her shoulders. She'd explained how she had somehow needed it and how calm she'd felt afterwards. That was what he was hoping to do to her tonight and he had to remain strong enough to deliver a punishment hard enough to give her what she so badly needed.

He helped her to her feet then pulled her into his arms, holding her tightly until he felt her stiff body relax against him.

"I love you," he whispered, nuzzling her hair. *Oh God, I love her more than life itself.* She was the most precious person in his life and yet here he was, about to put her through a grueling corporal punishment that would make her scream from the pain that he was going to inflict. He was going to take no pleasure from this.

"Frankie, you don't have to go ahead with this," he said suddenly. He knew she needed it, but he would never forgive himself if he had somehow misread the situation and he did more harm than good.

She blinked away a tear that had pooled in one of her eyes and he watched it roll down her check. "I know, Master, but I deserve this punishment and I want to take it for you."

"It's not just for me, though, it's got to be for you too. Can you see that?"

She smiled and nodded. "Yes, Master, I can. I know what it is you're trying to do and you're right. I need this. Please, Sir, give me the punishment I deserve."

"All right, but promise me you'll use your safe word if it gets too much," he said gruffly, trying to sound more confident than he felt.

"I promise, Master."

He nodded before turning to his toy bag that was on the floor nearby. Rummaging inside he pulled out what he needed then held them out for Frankie to see. The blood drained from her face when she saw the wooden paddle and the dreaded flogger that she hated so much. This was it. He just hoped that he was doing the right thing.

At the sight of the paddle and flogger that Jake had just pulled out of his bag, Frankie nearly said her safe word there and then. He hadn't been joking when he'd said it would be intense. *Shit!*

That paddle was nasty. It was made from hard wood with holes in the middle to make it move faster through the air, thereby giving it a hefty whack. But it was the flogger that really caught her attention. *Bloody hell.* The last time he'd used that she'd had to call her safe word before he'd even gotten properly started. It had looked almost pretty at first but it was the most painful flogger she'd ever experienced. She'd rather have the single tail whip than that thing.

"Go and stand by the St. Andrew's Cross," ordered Jake, once again sounding like the stern Dom she was used to.

It would have been so easy to have backed out when he'd said she didn't have to go through with it, but that wasn't what she wanted. Deep down, although she knew this was going to hurt, she needed to feel that pain. She needed it to punish her and release her. Jake knew it too.

"Stand facing the cross and hold on to the top of each arm. Spread your legs so they're flush with the cross."

She did as Jake had ordered and waited for him to attach the cuffs. Except she wasn't wearing any cuffs. So how was he going to restrain her?

"I'm going to make this harder for you, Frankie," said Jake as he walked up behind her. He stroked her right arm lightly and kissed the back of her neck sending, goosebumps tingling along her skin. "There will be no bondage to keep you in place. It'll be up to you to maintain your position. Keep a firm grip on the top of the cross and make sure your legs remain spread. Every time you move out of position, you'll be denied an orgasm."

Bastard! "Yes, Master."

She gripped the top arms of the cross as tightly as she could, determined not to let go at any cost. Then she waited for his hand to stroke her arse, to gently wake up the nerve endings before he would spank her lightly to warm her skin. The piercing crack that bounced off the walls took her completely by surprise, but not as much as the searing pain across her buttocks. *Fuck!*

The paddle hit again, blistering her unsuspecting skin and forcing a gasp from her. Oh God, that really hurt. He hit her left buttock, then her thigh, then back to the sore spot he'd hit a moment ago. The pain was excruciating as the paddle crashed against the back of her leg, but it was when it returned to her bottom and hit the same spot over and over that she honestly thought he had set it alight. The flames licked her skin as the scorching heat intensified on that one spot. Finally, when she didn't think she could take another direct hit, she couldn't help moving her body to the side to avoid the next blow.

"Get back in position," barked Jake.

She groaned. Was that the first orgasm she'd lost? She reluctantly moved back to the center and repositioned herself, praying silently that he wouldn't hit that same spot again. Before she could brace herself for the next impact, an almighty slap landed on her right buttock. Thank God he had changed sides, but for how long? The paddle continued beating her right cheek until that one burned as fiercely as the left.

"Ow, ow, ow!"

"Accept the pain, Frankie." As he spoke he landed another blindingly hard smack on her smoldering arse, and she screamed. This was torturous. There was nothing sensual about this—just relentless, agonizing pain. Was she finding release through the pain? No, she felt nothing except the fire that raged behind her. This wasn't how she'd hoped it would be, it wasn't working. She tasted a salty tear that ran into her mouth just as she opened it to let out another scream. *I can't do this.*

"Frankie?"

It took a moment to register that Jake was speaking to her. At least he'd stopped hitting her with that damned paddle.

She opened her eyes and looked into the blurry image of his face. He wiped her tears and the image sharpened.

"Are you okay?"

She hiccupped and nodded. Her arse felt like it had been scorched by a red hot poker, but otherwise she was intact.

"Do you want to use your safe word?"

She shook her head. "No, Master." She'd damn well show him she could take this.

"Okay. I'm going to use the flogger now. You'd better brace yourself, Frankie, this is going to hurt." His voice was deep and gruff. He meant it.

Suddenly she wasn't so sure that she was okay after all. Her legs were weak as they trembled under her and she felt sick with dread. She'd barely been able to take the pain of the paddle, how the hell was she going to cope with the flogger? She knew there would come a point where her body could no longer deal with the pain and that that would be her escape. But to get to the point where her mind would detach itself from her body, she would have to endure far more than she already had. She had to do this.

And anyway, she deserved this punishment as much as she needed it. She would take it with as much dignity as she could muster and when it was over, Jake would hold her and everything would be all right again.

Chapter Fifteen

Frankie tried to steady her breathing as she anticipated the first lash of the demon flogger. Her legs trembled beneath her and her body shivered. The dungeon was warm so why did she feel so cold?

Her bottom still burned from the paddling and she knew that every hit with the flogger would be so much more intense because of it. What the hell had she agreed to? Was she mad? Before she could answer herself a hard blow landed across the backs of her thighs.

She screamed from the shock of the pain. She was aware that Jake hadn't hit her anywhere near as hard as he usually would with a flogger and yet the pain was so much worse. It was an evil pain, one that not only hurt like hell when the fronds landed, but that left a burning sting in its wake.

He hit her again, only this time on her upper back. The physical distance between the impacts confused her body and her breath hitched. The pain wasn't quite as intense as it had been on her thighs, though, and she was silently grateful for the small mercy.

But then she felt as if a dozen bees had stung her arse when the flogger landed heavily across her buttocks. The pain gripped her around the throat and restricted her breathing as she tried to process it. She gasped sharply when she was finally able to take in some air. It hit again and again and the few bees quickly became a swarm of angry wasps on the attack. The swarm grew bigger with each stinging lash and the pain just kept getting worse and more overpowering.

Why wasn't she going to her special place? Why didn't the pain become a warm and comforting part of her the way she'd thought it would? Actually, the pain was changing, but it wasn't the sensation she'd been hoping for. A hard, icy ball was forming in the pit of her stomach that seemed to feed off the agony being inflicted on her. With every excruciating lash the ball got bigger. The fire on her skin didn't seem to melt the ball's icy core, but only made everything inside her feel colder.

She almost choked as a deep sob managed to escape from the hell inside her and, once that was released, another sought its freedom followed quickly by another. The tears continued to fall, burning her cheeks as if they were acid, but she couldn't stop them.

As if that wasn't bad enough, a new pain then joined the swarm attacking her skin, but this pain came from deep within. It seeped into the ball that continued to grow inside her and spread to her heart. She closed her eyes to try to blot out the unwelcome feelings, but the darkness only made it much scarier.

Another harsh lash landed across her back and she screamed. Why wasn't the pain making her feel better? Why did she feel as if her heart was shattering into a million pieces? She opened her eyes then shut them tightly again in the hope that the darkness would be gone, but instead she saw the face of a baby and her heart broke all over again. As the face started fading, so did any momentary hope that it was real. *Nooo, don't take away my baby.* The image disappeared leaving Frankie with a crushing despair that gripped her heart and squeezed until the little shards of ice around it started to crack. A piece of the ice fell away, tumbling into a bottomless lake, then another. Like an avalanche, once the first of the ice started tumbling, the rest was unstoppable.

Great racking sobs shook her body as she finally felt the grief she hadn't been able to deal with when she had lost the baby. It was all her fault. Maybe she'd eaten something bad without thinking, or maybe she been working too hard. Or, maybe the playful spanking Jake had given her the day before had started it all. Maybe their baby had died because of their stupid kinky games.

She hadn't noticed that the flogging had stopped until she let go of the cross and started to fall. Strong arms caught her and held her tight, but there was no comfort in them. The ball that had consumed her during the flogging suddenly exploded, sending little daggers of rage out through her pores and aimed straight at Jake.

"No," she screamed, scrambling desperately to get out of Jake's grip. "Get away from me."

"Shh, sweetheart, it's all right. Let it all out." His voice was soothing, which only fueled her anger.

How dare he be so calm when her world was shattering around her? With a strength she didn't know she possessed she pushed against Jake's chest and wriggled out of his arms. The black rage now turned a dangerous shade of red, and Jake was right in the firing line. Bunching her hands into tight fists, she launched at him, hammering at his chest as hard as she could.

"You don't care that our baby died. You don't care," she screamed, pummeling at him with every ounce of her strength. She wanted him to suffer like she had. She'd make him feel the despair that had been eating away at her ever since it had happened.

The fury tore through her like a tornado, ripping all the anguish from her heart and hurling it in Jake's direction. All the pent-up anger and sorrow that had haunted her for the last two years was being released in the storm that continued to batter him.

But, gradually, the fury drained out of her and her onslaught slowed. She was vaguely aware of the shocked expression on Jake's ashen face as she stepped away from him. *Oh God, what's happening to me?* She needed to get away from him, away from the pain. She grabbed a folded robe from a dresser nearby, slipped it on without thinking too much about what she was doing and ran out of the room.

She didn't know where she was going or even why she was running, all she knew was that she needed to get away from the agony that was consuming her. She ran until something solid blocked her path. Strong hands gripped her arms, stopping her from running any farther.

"Frankie."

She was vaguely aware of someone saying her name. Not Jake's voice.

"Frankie."

This time the voice registered in her head and she managed to snap out of the fog clouding her mind.

"Marco?"

"What happened, petal?" asked Marco, not letting go of her.

"I... I don't..." she faltered. How the hell could she even begin to tell Marco about her outburst and what lay behind it? Hell, she couldn't even make sense of it herself.

"Where's Jake?" he asked with a note of concern in his voice.

"In the dungeon," she replied as if on autopilot.

"Let me take you back before—"

"No!" She pulled away from Marco and glared at him. "I don't want to see him."

Panic surged through her at the thought of being taken back to the dungeon. Back to where all her pain had come to such a dramatic head. She couldn't face that. Or Jake. She backed away from Marco, ready to flee.

Marco seemed to sense her intention to run because he took her hand in a firm grip, stopping her escape.

"Listen to me," he said urgently. "Don't worry, you don't have to go back there but I need to get a message to Jake to let him know you're with me. Okay?"

She nodded. She was drained, numb. There was no fight left in her.

Still holding onto her hand, Marco took his phone out of his pocket, punched in some numbers then spoke quietly. She didn't try to listen to what he was saying, she didn't even know to whom he spoke. When he put his phone away again he said, "Ross, one of the Dungeon Monitors, is going to let Jake know you're with me."

She nodded again and tried to stop her body from swaying. The corridor seemed to be spinning, her vision was blurred.

The next thing she knew she was being carried through a private kitchen and into a small courtyard garden. She blinked and took a deep breath.

The air was unusually warm for the time of year and smelled of grass and autumn flowers. She took in a few more breaths as Marco carried her across the courtyard toward a covered archway with a swing seat tucked neatly under it. Still remaining silent, he carefully lowered her onto the seat then sat down next to her.

"Where are we?" she whispered, unable to contain her curiosity despite the myriad of emotions raging inside her head.

"We're in my private garden," he said, softly.

"Oh."

He didn't say anything else and she was grateful. He had every right to demand why she'd been running away from Jake but he just silently held onto her, rocking gently in the giant swing seat. The motion soothed her and his calm presence made her feel safe. She closed her eyes in the hope that the pain gnawing at her heart would go away, but of course it didn't. In fact it just got worse as images of her dead baby flashed across her closed eyelids.

"My baby," she whispered, as a fresh tear rolled down her cheek. "I want my baby back."

"I know," said Marco softly and gently stroked her hair. "I know."

Then, finally, the grief that had been locked away in her heart for so long was set free. The grief that she hadn't been able to share with anyone, even Jake. She'd pushed him away, too afraid of losing her mind if she allowed herself to express her sorrow.

"Oh God," she cried as a dark and heavy cloud overwhelmed her. Suddenly the tears broke through and tumbled down her hot face as her heart fractured the remaining ice that had clung to it. It felt as if it broke over and over again as her body shook with the tears that came from within it and every tear carried the despair that had weighed her down for so long.

She cried until she thought there were no tears left, but then another wave of helplessness smothered her and a fresh barrage of grief was released.

Marco held her in his arms the whole time and let her cry until the flow of tears started to slow, leaving her feeling drained and empty. When they stopped completely, she slumped into Marco's arms too exhausted to move or say anything. She didn't need to. Marco understood and just let her cling to him for as long as she needed to. Finally, though, she pulled away and looked at him, blinking back the residual tears still lurking behind her eyes.

"I'm sorry," she hiccupped.

"Don't be," replied Marco, his deep voice soothing her fraught emotions. "You've needed that release for a long time and I'm glad you were finally able to let it go."

"Oh God," she groaned when the memory of her outburst at Jake hit her like a thunderbolt. She'd attacked him and accused him of not caring about the death of their baby. She hadn't meant it. She'd just needed to release her suppressed turmoil and he'd been the obvious victim. But, although she knew that he had grieved in his own way, she still couldn't understand how he had been able to get on with his life as if nothing had happened. He'd written his best book in the aftermath and had reveled in its success.

Then there was his eagerness to resume their D/s relationship. Why would he want that so badly when it could very well have been responsible for her losing their baby?

As if reading her mind, Marco rubbed her cheek with his coarse thumb then turned her head to face him and commanded her full attention.

"Jake asked me if the kink might have had anything to do with your baby dying," he said, solemnly. "He told me that you'd focused mainly on the D/s element of the lifestyle since discovering you were pregnant and a very light spanking was as heavy as it got where impact play was concerned."

Frankie nodded. In fact, the spanking he'd given her the day before she'd miscarried had been so light that she'd been frustrated and had asked him to hit her harder. He'd refused and she'd been pissed off with him.

"That's not enough to harm a baby, you know," he said, gently. "Whatever the reason it happened, you mustn't blame the kink."

"I know," she whispered. "Jake must hate me."

"Of course he doesn't. He adores you, Frankie."

She laughed bitterly. "Yeah, right. I attacked him, accused him of not caring about what happened then abandoned him."

"You needed to let go of your emotions. I think you needed to be away from him to do that. You both needed a little time away from each other, but now you've got to talk to him. Tell him how you feel, that you don't blame the kink but equally, if you do harbor any grievances you need to get it out in the open, clear the air. And listen to what he's got to say as well. He was devastated, Frankie. You weren't the only one who suffered."

Marco spoke evenly, but his words exploded in her head as if they had been armed with dynamite. '*Talk to him... Clear the air... He was devastated.'* At that moment, she didn't know what she was going to say to him.

"Yes, you're right... I just don't know what to think right now. God, I'm so screwed up."

She leaned into Marco and buried her head in his chest. He was so strong, so warm, so safe. Just like Jake. He held her firmly as he continued to rock gently and her body relaxed into his. She was so tired. Her body felt heavy, her heart numb. How was she going to get through this? Thank God for Jake. She needed her husband's love, his forgiveness so she lifted her head and brushed her lips against his. She kissed him, slipping her tongue into his mouth and waited for his hard, dominating response. Suddenly the only thing that mattered was that kiss. In it, she sought solace, comfort. She so badly needed Jake and to make things right with him again.

"Frankie, no. You're my friend's wife and I won't betray either of you. You're in no frame of mind to know what you're doing right now."

Frankie pulled away and stared at Marco in shock as she realized her mistake. "I... I'm sorry. I thought you were..."

Marco didn't look phased, though, and stood up. Taking her hand, he helped her to stand. "Don't worry, I know you were confused. Come on, I'm taking you up to your room. You need to get some sleep because you've got a lot of talking to do with your husband when you wake up."

She allowed him to lead her back through the kitchen and into a small hallway that looked like the entrance to a private flat. She remained silent as he walked her up the main staircase and toward her room.

When they reached it he opened the door with a master key card and gently nudged her to go in.

"Will you be all right?"

Ha, that's the question of the century. She nodded. "Yes, thank you."

"Okay. I'll let Jake know where you are. Try to get some sleep." He kissed the top of her head, then turned to walk away.

"Marco?"

He turned and raised his eyebrows. He didn't seem to show any of the awkwardness that she was feeling.

"I'm sorry. About before. You know…"

He smiled, his dark eyes softening as he replied, "Don't worry about it. It's forgotten already. Goodnight."

"Goodnight," she whispered as she watched him walk away.

She closed the door and walked slowly toward the bed. Where was Jake? What must he be thinking right now? Why had she kissed Marco? Her head spun with questions all jumbling together to make it hurt. Her heart was heavy as she slumped onto the plump duvet. She wanted to cry, but she was all cried out. She was empty.

She managed to maneuver her exhausted body under the duvet, but resolved to remain awake until Jake returned to their room. But lying on her back brought back some of the pain from the flogging so she rolled onto her front and snuggled farther into the duvet, seeking its warmth and comfort. Her eyes stung from all the crying so she closed them to give them a rest. She wouldn't sleep, she mustn't. There was so much they needed to talk about and so much she needed to think about. She would use this quiet time to think and when he returned they'd talk. She needed to think. What was it she needed to think about? Her thoughts became cloudy as she gave up the fight to stay awake and finally fell into a deep and troubled sleep.

Chapter Sixteen

Jake poured himself a generous glass of whiskey in the private bar. His hand shook as he lifted it and took a large swig. He was still reeling from Frankie's outburst. *That wasn't meant to happen.* As the liquid burned its way to his stomach, he welcomed the soothing warmth and quickly took another mouthful.

He had a vague recollection of one of the Dungeon Monitors checking on him in the dungeon and letting him know that Frankie was safe with Marco. But he had no memory of coming to the bar. Nor did he have any idea how long he'd been here, staring numbly into the roaring fire before deciding that he needed a drink. The only thing he was aware of was Frankie's words. *'You don't care.'*

He laughed bitterly and poured the last of the drink down his throat. Well, he'd wanted to send her to subspace so she could finally let go and exorcise her demons and she sure as hell had done that.

When she'd started crying during the flogging he'd been able to tell it was more than just the usual reaction to the pain. The sobs had shaken her entire body and had sounded heartbreakingly desperate. At that moment he'd thought he'd broken through and that all he'd needed to do was hold her while she cried it all out. Then they'd have talked and everything would have been good again. How wrong he'd been.

He poured himself another glass, this time filling it almost to the top. *So now what?* Where did they go from here? Was there anywhere to go from here?

The door clicked softly and he glanced up to see Marco enter, looking as solemn as he felt.

"She's gone to bed," said Marco, walking over to join him at the bar.

Jake reached for another glass and poured his friend an equally large amount of the high-quality whiskey. Marco took the crystal tumbler and sat down on a stool next to him.

"How is she?" asked Jake.

"Exhausted," replied Marco quietly. "She had two years' worth of grief to expel."

"She hates me." Even saying the words out loud cut Jake to pieces.

But Marco shook his head. "No, mate. She doesn't, but she needed an outlet for release and you were it."

"I'm not sure if we can ever get over this," said Jake. For the first time since they'd arrived at Dominion, he genuinely doubted his future with Frankie. It seemed hopeless now.

"Of course you will, but you need to talk to her. And it's not just Frankie that has to open up, you've got to tell her how you feel. It seems to me that you both refused to face what happened at the time. Yes, Frankie sought refuge in her business, but you wrote your book. I'll bet you haven't shed any tears, right?"

Jake shrugged.

"You're as bad as each other." Marco finished his drink then stood up. "I need to check on the guests, there are a few still playing. Stay in here for as long as you need."

"Thanks," mumbled Jake without looking up.

When he was alone again, Jake walked back to the fireplace and settled himself into a large, high-backed leather armchair directly in front of the warm glow. The ticking of the clock made the calm stillness of the room seem more palpable with only the crackle of the fire adding to the soft cadence.

Staring into the fire, he tried to put his thoughts into some sort of cohesive order. He'd check on Frankie in a bit, but first he needed to sort his head out.

'You don't care.' Did she really think that? It was easy for Marco to say she didn't, but he couldn't really know.

A piece of wood suddenly flared up, spitting out little sparks and throwing orange shadows across the room. As the flames settled back down again, he thought about what Marco had said. He'd been uncomfortably close to the mark.

He couldn't deny that he'd tried to bury his own pain by focusing so intensely on his book. Its success had been bittersweet. He had gained no pleasure from the generous royalty payments or rave reviews, but had used the achievement as a screen to hide behind. He'd done exactly the same thing that Frankie had done. Marco was right—they really were as bad as each other.

Except he hadn't accused Frankie of not caring. He could have dealt with Frankie's outburst and would have helped her through it, but now, knowing she hated him and thought that he was some cold-hearted

193

bastard, he really couldn't see how they could ever recover from this.

'*You don't care.*' He downed the rest of the whiskey, his eyes watering as it burned inside him. His hopes of ever being happy again shattered before him as the cloak of misery that was wrapping itself around his heart started to feel like it might suffocate him. How ironic that in bringing Frankie here to try to save their relationship he'd ended up driving the final nail into the coffin.

As he continued staring into the fire, a vision of Frankie's haunted face appeared, taunting him with an angry, accusatory glare. He closed his eyes to escape the image jumping out at him from the smoldering embers and allowed the empty glass in his hand to fall to the floor. It landed with a blunt thud on the soft carpet and that was the last thing he remembered as he lost the battle with the darkness and fell asleep.

* * * *

Someone was shining a torch into Frankie's eyes. She squeezed them shut and attempted to block out the brightness trying to force its way through her eyelids, but the light wouldn't go away. She tentatively opened one eye then quickly shut it again when she saw the light was coming from the window. A bright beam of sunshine had settled directly across her pillow. Jake must have got up early and opened the curtains. Instead of yesterday's spark of annoyance, though, a strange sense of foreboding crept into her heart. Something wasn't right.

She sat up and tried to focus on her surroundings. Jake wasn't in the room. The bathroom door was open and the room was empty. *Where is he? Maybe he's gone for an early morning run?*

She slid toward the edge of the bed and winced as the sheet rubbed against her bottom. *Bloody hell, that must have been some scene last night. Last night. What happened last night?* She shook her head and rubbed her eyes. Something told her that she needed to wake up properly because all was not well.

A flashback of pain striking her back, legs and arse sent a jolt through her body. *Oh yes, my punishment.* It had really hurt. She had tried to seek refuge in her own padded world of pleasure, but all she'd felt was relentless pain. But the pain had come from within. She was starting to remember. But the more her thoughts came back into focus the more she didn't want them to.

Oh fuck. Her breakdown—it was all coming back to her now. She didn't know what the hell had come over her as she had screamed and hit out at Jake. She'd had no control of her body or her words. It was as if someone else had possessed her and left her helplessly watching in the background. What was it she'd said to him? She was struggling to remember the actual words, they seemed to be surrounded by fog.

Anger! That's what she'd felt. Anger and sorrow. Her beautiful baby. Hazy snippets started to jump out at her. *'I want my baby back.'* The pain returned like a sharp slap to her face and tears burned her sore eyes. She'd cried for her lost baby.

'You don't care.' Why did those words keep ringing in her ears? Who didn't care? She heard her own voice screaming the accusation, but why? Then, Jake's shocked expression flashed before her and everything came back with stark clarity. She'd finally told him

how upset she was that he didn't seem that bothered about what had happened to their baby. She hadn't meant it come out like that though. *Oh God, what have I done?*

Before she could fully comprehend what had happened, another vision popped into her head. Marco. There had been a garden of some sort, fresh air. And a swing seat. She'd kissed Marco.

What the hell is happening to me? And where's Jake? Maybe he'd found out about her attempt at kissing Marco? Or maybe he despised her for her hateful words. She wouldn't blame him.

She needed to find him. She had to explain why she'd blown up like that, and they needed to talk so they could clear the air once and for all. But was it too late? Had he already left?

Suddenly, an overwhelming sense of urgency made her jump off the bed. She had to find Jake. She grabbed some jogging pants and a T-shirt before putting them on as fast as she could. She didn't even bother to check her face or hair, the only thing that mattered was finding Jake.

She slipped her shoes on and ran out of the room, not caring if she had her key card or not. The house was quiet. It was probably still early and knowing the nature of the weekend, most people would still be asleep. She ran down the stairs and hesitated when she got to the bottom. Where was the most likely place he'd be? Surely he wouldn't still be in the dungeon? No, it was more likely he'd be outside somewhere.

She started running toward the main entrance hall, turned a corner and ran straight into someone. *Christina!*

"Hey, slow down," laughed Christina, grabbing Frankie's arm to steady her.

"Sorry," panted Frankie. "I need to find Jake." There was no time for a girly chit-chat now. She needed to get away from Christina so she could find Jake. She pulled away from Christina's grip and looked around her desperately. *Where is he?*

"Frankie, calm down." A shadow of concern crossed Christina's face as she appeared to study Frankie. "You look terrible, honey. Are you okay?"

Frankie forced a bright smile onto her face. "Yes, I'm fine..." Then she faltered as the sense of urgency that had driven her a moment ago turned to dread. She wasn't so sure all of a sudden that she wanted to find Jake because then he might very well tell her that he was leaving her. She couldn't bear that. He was everything to her. Everything. She couldn't lose him now. She stared at Christina through fresh tears, not knowing what to do or say.

"No, you're not." Christina took her hand and led her down the corridor in the direction of the back of the house. "What's wrong?" she asked as they passed the staircase.

"I... I had a bit of a meltdown last night," said Frankie, wondering how on earth she could put what had happened into words. She didn't want to go into detail, though, mainly because she needed to talk to Jake first. She decided to leave out the whole sorry story of the punishment and her subsequent attack on Jake. "Basically, Jake and I had an argument. Then I kissed Marco." She withdrew her hand from Christina's and braced herself for an outraged reaction.

Christina stopped dead in her tracks. "Bloody hell," she muttered. "Come on, let's go somewhere private where we can talk." She tried the handle of the door they'd stopped by but it was locked. Grabbing

Frankie's hand again, Christina led her toward the next door. This one opened. She quickly pulled Frankie inside and shut the door firmly.

"What did you mean by that?" demanded Christina. "Did you actually make a pass it him?"

Frankie sighed. "He was being so kind. He held me in his arms and it felt good. Then I kissed him but I thought he was... Oh, Christina, what have I done?"

Before Christina could answer, though, the sound of movement from across the room made them both turn around. If Frankie had thought before that things couldn't get any worse she'd been wrong. Because standing in front of the fireplace, with a face like thunder, was Jake.

Chapter Seventeen

What? Had Frankie really just said that she'd made a pass at Marco? Jake shook his head, but it remained fuzzy. He'd been awakened by the sound of the door to the bar closing then by Christina's insistent voice. At first he hadn't realized she'd been talking to Frankie—it was only when his wife's voice had shakily confessed her guilty secret that the implications of their conversation had become clear.

What was he doing in here anyway? The last thing he remembered was staring into the fire as he'd struggled to come to terms with Frankie's outburst. He must have fallen asleep. And now he'd woken to hear Frankie telling Christina that she'd slept with Marco. He was sure that was what she'd just said.

He stared speechlessly at Frankie and Christina's shocked faces. Nobody said anything. The tension buzzed between them like sparks from a broken live wire. Even in his floored state, though, he couldn't blame Frankie. She'd been broken last night and wouldn't have known what she was doing. But Marco...

Anger flared through him with a force that threatened to destroy his control. No fucking wonder Marco had been so quick to help him out by taking Frankie back to her room.

Had he fucked her before he'd come down to the bar or had he gone back up to their room after their chat and taken advantage of Frankie's distressed state? A lethal cocktail of hatred and betrayal squeezed his heart painfully. It was one thing to share her in a controlled BDSM scene, but for Marco to seduce her without his permission or knowledge crossed a line drawn in blood. Rage bubbled up inside him, simmering just below the surface like a volcano about to erupt. He was going to fucking kill him.

With a deep growl, he stormed past Frankie and Christina, who remained rooted to the spot in shock, and grabbed the doorknob. The damned door wouldn't open, his hand was shaking too much to grip the handle properly.

"Jake…" started Frankie, with a strange high-pitched edge to her voice.

Luckily the door finally did open and he was able to escape before Frankie could speak again. He didn't want to hear anything she had to say right now, at least not until he had sorted Marco out.

He knew where he'd find him. Marco had always been an early riser, even in his all-night partying rock star days, and loved the silent peace of the outdoors as the sun rose in the sky. That told him all he needed to know.

His rage gathered momentum with each angry stride. By the time he reached the side door leading out to the gardens, a red film had settled before his eyes and the rage had turned into murderous fury. It didn't take long to spot Marco, practicing his morning tai chi on a large, open lawn. Jake's pace quickened as he neared. Then his eyes locked onto his target through the red haze as he launched himself forward as if he were an armed missile.

Marco looked up just in time to see him approach and lifted an arm in automatic self-defense as Jake threw himself at him.

"You bastard," roared Jake as he threw a heavy punch in the direction of Marco's face.

The red fog blurred his vision as he lashed out at his new foe. As he pounded blindly at Marco using every last bit of his strength, the rage seemed to take on a life of its own. He had no idea whether Marco was defending himself or throwing punches back at him, all he could see and feel was the demonic force that had possessed him the way a malevolent spirit might.

As he unleashed his anger savagely on Marco, though, Jake started to become vaguely aware that something new was taking hold of him. Somehow, oddly, the anger was turning into a sharp pain stabbing fiercely at his heart, harder and deeper with its every beat.

The two men rolled on the ground as if they were unleashed Rottweilers trained to fight to the death. But the only thing Jake was aware of now was grief as the steel armor was ripped from around his heart. Then he heard an anguished cry, almost like the howl of an injured animal. It sounded strangely as if it had come from inside himself. Suddenly, as if the sound had somehow emitted a subliminal signal, all the fight drained out of him. He collapsed on top of Marco and, to his horror, the river of sorrow that had flowed through his life in the past two years burst its banks.

Jake was not a man who cried easily, but now he seemed unable to stop the torrent of despair pouring out of him. The anguish that had clung to him for such a long time was finally stripped away exposing his heart to raw feelings that he wasn't sure he could deal with.

Slowly, though, he began to regain his composure. He gradually became aware that he was sitting on the grass next to Marco, feeling numb. A quick glance at Marco told him that he hadn't done too much damage. A small trickle of blood ran from his nose and his right eye was red and puffy, but that seemed a small price to pay for his betrayal. Yet the anger was gone and, oddly enough, so was the weight that had held him down for so long.

"Are you finished?" asked Marco, wiping away the blood from his nose.

"Yeah," grunted Jake.

"Good, because we need to talk."

"There's nothing to talk about," growled Jake. *What bullshit – there's plenty to fucking talk about.* He didn't want to hear what Marco had to say.

"I don't need to be a mind reader to guess what this is about. Nothing happened between me and Frankie," said Marco, brushing flattened grass off his green stained white T-shirt.

"Oh really?" retorted Jake, bitterly. "So you don't consider sleeping with my wife to be anything significant?"

"What?" Marco's look of surprise matched the intonation in his voice. "What exactly did she tell you?"

Jake opened his mouth to reply then shut it again as he tried to recall exactly what it was Frankie had said. Something about how nice it had felt being held in Marco's arms, then she'd kissed him and... And what? What had she said?

"Jake, I don't know what you think you heard, but I can assure you that nothing untoward happened between Frankie and me. She was upset, as you know, and I comforted her. That's it."

"She kissed you," snapped Jake.

Marco actually laughed. "Yeah, but a kiss is hardly a criminal offense. She was distraught and was momentarily caught off guard. She needed you at that moment and thought I was *you*. It didn't go any further and, just for the record, she was mortified."

Jake was silent as he absorbed Marco's words. She had kissed him, but that was all. Marco was a man of truth, of that there was no doubt. If he said nothing had happened then it hadn't. Marco was so damned honest that he wouldn't have hesitated in giving him the brutal truth, no matter how hard that would have been to hear.

So Marco hadn't betrayed his friendship and Frankie hadn't been unfaithful. The mere fact that she felt so bad about a stolen kiss was testament to her loyalty to him. If he'd really thought about it, he would have known that she'd never cheat on him. The same went for Marco. Of course he'd never do the dirty on a mate, he just wasn't like that. What the hell was wrong with him? Why had he flown off the handle like that instead of thinking rationally before charging in like a fucking brain-dead bull?

Fuck, he'd screwed up. Again. Not only had he just made Frankie feel even worse about herself, but he'd just beaten one of his best friends up. Well, maybe not. Marco was tough and could easily have knocked him out if he'd wanted to. Jake had a feeling that he'd barely have felt the punches he'd thrown at him.

"I'm sorry," mumbled Jake, fully aware that his feeble apology wouldn't excuse his attack on Marco.

Had he just lost a good friend? And what about Frankie? Where did they go from here?

"Forget it," said Marco, grinning sheepishly at Jake. "Although I think you need some boxing lessons."

Despite everything, Jake smiled. *Yeah, okay, I'm not exactly Rambo.* "I jumped to the wrong conclusion. I'm an idiot."

"Yeah, but you just did something that might very well have saved your relationship," said Marco, thoughtfully.

Jake frowned, not sure what Marco was getting at.

Marco shrugged then continued, "You did what Frankie did last night. You cried. You finally allowed your feelings to come out through the tears that you both needed to shed. Now there's nothing left to stop you from rebuilding the bond that you had before."

"She thinks I don't care about the baby," said Jake quietly. Her words from last night still rang in his ears.

"For crying out loud," snapped Marco, beginning to sound frustrated. "Talk. To. Her. Make her understand how you felt at the time and tell her that she'd fucking better start talking to you as well."

If they'd only talked instead of burying themselves in their work this whole sorry mess would never have happened. They should have cried together, shared their grief and recovered with their mutual support. He'd bet she'd been going through similar feelings of anguish and conflict at the time. He remembered not wanting her to see him upset because it might have made her feel worse. Had she thought the same thing? The mere thought broke his heart all over again. Fuck, what had they been thinking?

She had had so much to deal with, and here he was demanding things of her that he had no right to demand. He'd hoped that by bringing her here and asking her to submit, some of the ice surrounding her heart would melt away and draw them close again, but he'd been wrong. He'd tried using BDSM, but it hadn't worked. So, was this it?

With a heavy heart he stood up and brushed himself down. Marco was right about one thing. He and Frankie did need to talk, but he feared that it wouldn't be the conversation he'd been hoping for. He'd been a fool for thinking that bringing out her submissive side again would make everything all right. Instead, he'd made things worse.

"I'm sorry," he said quietly to Marco. "About everything." With a curt nod at him, he turned then walked slowly back to the house.

* * * *

"Frankie, calm down. He won't do anything stupid." Christina didn't look as sure of that as she sounded, though.

"I've never seen him look so angry," said Frankie, running a hand worriedly through her hair the way she always did when she was upset.

"Why don't you go after him?" asked Christina, reaching for the door handle.

"No." Frankie stepped away from the door as if she thought Christina might try to push her out.

"Why? What's wrong? There's more to this than you kissing Marco, isn't there?" Christina put her arm around her and walked her across the room to the sofa. "Sit down."

Frankie slumped into the deep, plush sofa. She hid her face in her hands, shaking her head as a feeling of hopelessness swamped her. Christina sat down next to her, but didn't say anything. Frankie was glad of the silence as she tried to find the words to explain what had happened.

"We had a row," she finally said, her voice barely a whisper. "I said some terrible things." She looked up at Christina through the blur of tears flooding her eyes, "I couldn't deal with the pain, you see."

Christina frowned. "Pain? You mean from your scene? Why didn't you use your safe word?"

Frankie shook her head. "No, not that kind of pain. Two years ago I had a miscarriage. I was eleven weeks pregnant."

"Oh, honey, I'm so sorry." Christina threw her arms around Frankie and hugged her close.

Frankie held onto her, glad of her friend's warm comfort. Christina didn't press for details, she just offered her unconditional support in her silent embrace and Frankie was grateful for that.

Despite last night's release, the grief still hurt but, for the first time since it had happened, the pain wasn't trapped inside her heart. It seeped out in her tears and left her with an unfamiliar hint of relief.

When she finally felt able to speak without losing control, she pulled away from Christina slightly and looked at her. "I don't want to talk about the details of what happened, but, basically, last night I accused Jake of not caring about losing our baby," said Frankie, quietly. "That was a horrible thing to say."

"Yeah," replied Christina, bluntly. "Did you mean it?"

Frankie shook her head. "No, of course not. I knew deep down that he was sad, but I honestly believed he was dealing with it a lot better than I was. I felt that I needed to be just as strong as him, but I wasn't so I hid my feelings behind my work. I resented his strength and, as a result, we started to grow apart. I can see that now."

Christina reached out and took hold of her hand. Giving it a squeeze she said softly, "Honey, you need to tell him this."

"I know, but he'll never listen now that he thinks I've slept with Marco. Oh God, what do you think he's doing to him?"

Christina chuckled. "I wouldn't worry about Marco, he can look after himself." She put her arm around Frankie again and gave her a lopsided cuddle. "What exactly did happen last night? Did you sleep with Marco?"

"No," protested Frankie. "Like I said just before Jake appeared out of nowhere, I kissed him. But I wasn't thinking straight. My mind was so screwed up and I wrongly thought it was Jake I was kissing."

"So you're not secretly in love with Marco then?" asked Christina, with a smile.

"No. I like him, fancy him even, but Jake's the only man I love. I'd never cheat on him." Even as she said the words she wondered if she'd ever get the chance now to prove that to him.

"So what happened after you kissed him?" persisted Christina.

Frankie shrugged. "Nothing. He pushed me away and brought me to my senses. Thank goodness. I just wish I had a chance to say that before Jake heard us and got the wrong end of the stick."

"I wouldn't worry, honey, Marco will sort him out."

An uncomfortable injection of fear seeped through Frankie's blood. "That's what I'm worried about. I've never seen Jake so pissed off and I know Marco could be a deadly opponent. That doesn't bode well."

Christina smiled and stood up. "I didn't mean that. I meant Marco will tell him the truth and if Jake's got any sense he'll understand how and why it happened." She walked over to the bar and reached for a couple of glasses. "Fancy an orange juice?"

Frankie shook her head. The thought of eating or drinking anything turned her stomach. The only thing she wanted was Jake, but if he survived his brawl with Marco he might not want her anymore. An icy grip of fear squeezed her heart as the possibility of losing him became more real.

Christina poured herself a glass of juice and rejoined Frankie on the sofa.

"What if we can't sort it out?" whispered Frankie, sadly. "What if that was the last straw and he walks away from me?"

"Don't let that happen, honey. You know he loves you, that won't have changed since last night. Show him you love him back. Make him stay."

"How?" Somehow Frankie had a feeling that mere words wouldn't be enough. She needed a miracle now.

"Why did he bring you here this weekend? What was it he was ultimately hoping for?" asked Christina, sounding surprisingly wise for her young years.

"My submission," replied Frankie, slowly. "He'd hoped that if he could make me submit again I might open up to him. He gave me an ultimatum, Christina, I either come with him this weekend or he'd leave me. He didn't tell me it was a BDSM weekend, though, because he knew I wouldn't have come."

"He must really love you to have gone to so much trouble," said Christina softly. "So what can you do to show him how much you love him?"

Tears pooled in Frankie's eyes as she acknowledged that all Jake had ever wanted was her. He'd wanted his wife back, the warm, loving woman he'd married. The woman who turned to gooey mush when he ordered her to kneel for him. The woman who handed her control to him because she loved and trusted him with all her heart.

"I think I know," said Frankie and stood up quickly. "If you see him, tell him I'm in our room."

"Okay," said Christina. She rose and followed Frankie to the door. "Good luck."

"Thanks." Frankie gave Christina a quick peck on the cheek and let herself out of the bar. She needed to get back to their room as quickly as she could. If Jake was leaving he'd have to go up to get his stuff, she'd just have to make sure she was there first. Her steps quickened as her resolve strengthened. Jake had done everything so far to try to save their marriage – now it was her turn. She was damned if she was going to lose him now. They'd been through too much together.

She ran up the stairs, two steps at a time. When she reached their room she stopped and frowned. The door wasn't properly shut. Had she left the door ajar in her earlier haste or had Jake already been and left?

She pushed the door open and tentatively peeped in. "Hello?"

No answer. She looked around and nearly cried with relief when she saw his things were still there. He hadn't gone. She left the door ajar in case he didn't have his key card either and began to search frantically for the thing she hoped he wouldn't be able to walk away from. Then all she could do was wait.

* * * *

Jake frowned when he saw the door to their room was ajar. It was unlike Frankie to be so careless. Had she already left?

He pushed the door open and froze in stunned disbelief when he took in the sight in front of him.

Frankie was kneeling in the middle of the room, naked, her head bowed submissively. He closed the door quietly and, as he approached her, she lifted her arms to offer him the item resting in her upturned palms. Her collar.

Fuck, this was so not what he'd been expecting. She looked beautiful, so naturally submissive that his heart contracted painfully in his chest.

"Frankie, we need to talk," he said softly. He didn't take the collar being offered to him.

"Yes, Master." Her voice quivered, and his heart went out to her.

"Get up. Please."

God, she was making this so much harder. All he wanted to do was accept the collar and place it around her neck where it belonged. Only it didn't really belong there, did it? That was the problem. She was only doing this because she thought he expected it. But that wasn't enough. It had to come from her. She had to want it as much as he did and, as much as it hurt him to acknowledge it, he was pretty sure that she didn't really want it.

She finally raised her eyes to meet his and his breath caught in his throat when he saw the confusion and hurt reflected through the tears that were gathering in them. Without a word he walked across to the bed and picked up her bathrobe. Then he returned and gently took the collar from her trembling hands. Instead of fastening it around her neck as she was expecting, though, he carefully placed it on a nearby chair then draped the bathrobe over her shoulders.

"Frankie, we need to talk as equals. Please get up." Towering over her kneeling body made him instinctively want to dominate her. But he fought the urge and instead offered his hand to help her up.

A single tear escaped down her cheek as she slowly reached out and took his hand. Silently he led her across the room to the sofa in the bay window. He sat down and waited for her to join him. Instead she fell to her knees in front of him and placed her head in his lap. Suddenly he was torn. He loved it when she did that. It made him feel as if he were her whole world. But he couldn't—wouldn't—demand her submission anymore. They had to talk as husband and wife. Then and only then could they discuss the remote possibility of resuming their D/s dynamic. *Fuck, this is going to be much harder than I'd thought.*

Chapter Eighteen

"Frankie, get up. *Now!*"

The uncompromising order sent shivers through Frankie's fragile body. Then confusion clouded her mind as she looked up into his face hoping for guidance. What was he doing? He'd just used his Dom voice to get her attention and yet he seemed to be rejecting her submission in the same breath.

He sighed impatiently then cursed quietly as if she were some irritating child who wouldn't stop badgering him to get what she wanted.

Suddenly her desire to kneel before her Master evaporated and a flash of anger replaced her willingness to submit. How dare he mess with her mind like that? He'd brought her here to relearn the art of submission. And when he'd finally got what he'd wanted, he'd bloody rejected her. Tears of humiliation burned her eyes as she scrambled up off the floor. *Bastard!*

"Fuck you," she snarled and stormed toward the bathroom.

"Frankie…"

"Get lost," she spat, her tone laced with venom. Was this because he still believed she'd slept with Marco? *Well, fuck him if he isn't prepared to give me the benefit of the doubt.*

Just as she approached the bathroom door he grabbed her firmly by the arm and pulled her back. With a low growl he leaned over her and took her mouth, forcing it open with his tongue. The kiss was hard, plundering her with a passion that literally left her breathless. She couldn't pull away, couldn't refuse him as he held her prisoner in his grip.

Despite her outrage, she didn't have the strength to fight him and so she surrendered to his almost brutal assault. The fiery anger died as quickly as it had flared up and was now replaced with countless butterflies fluttering excitedly around in her stomach. Her body weakened as her bones turned to rubber. Damn him, this was exactly what he'd done two days ago when he'd first brought her here. That was to entice back her submission, so why was he doing this now if he didn't want it anymore?

Finally, he allowed her to come up for air and pulled away. She glared at him as he surveyed her with eyes that burned with passion and power. There was absolutely no doubt that she was looking into the face of a Dom – a Dom who was as aroused by that kiss as she was. She was suddenly more confused than ever as it occurred to her that maybe Jake did want her – and her submission. So why hadn't he accepted the gift she'd offered him just moments ago?

Still holding onto her arm, he guided her back to the sofa and pushed her firmly down to sit on it. He quickly sat next to her then took both her hands in his.

"Do you love me?" he asked, gazing intently at her.

"Yes," she replied without hesitation.

"That's all I need to know." He let go of her hands and pulled her into his arms. "That's a pretty good place to start."

"Start what?" she whispered, taking in a deep breath to draw in as much of his masculine scent as possible.

"Rebuilding our lives," he replied, his voice husky in her ear. "Together."

"Jake, I didn't sleep with Marco," she said, desperate for him to know she hadn't betrayed him.

"I know, sweetheart. I'm sorry about reacting like that. I was an idiot." He pulled away and tucked a stray lock of hair behind her ear, the way he always did when her wayward hair fell over her eyes. It was familiar and comforting, a sign that he still cared for her. "Come on, get dressed. We're going for a walk."

Frankie smiled. Every time she and Jake needed to discuss something important they usually went for a walk. They both found it was so much easier getting something off their chests when they took a stroll in the fresh air—somehow it cleared their heads and helped the flow of words.

She nodded and stood, taking his hand when he held it out to her. A couple of minutes later she was dressed and ready.

She already felt more at ease as they made their way down the stairs and toward the side door leading to the gardens. It was still early and the house remained quiet and deserted. A random thought suddenly struck her as they walked past the door to the bar that Christina had dragged her through earlier. *What was Christina doing up so early?* She'd still been wearing last night's outfit—well, most of it. Frankie had been too absorbed in her own problems to ask her what she'd been doing up at that hour. She quickly forgot about Christina, though, as they neared the back door.

As they stepped outside she took in a gulp of the fresh morning air. The sun was up, shining onto fallen autumn leaves that twinkled with the dew that blanketed them. There was even a hint of optimism in the morning birdsong. Or was that just her imagination?

"Before we go any further," said Jake as they headed toward the woods at the far end of the vast lawn, "I want you to know that I do appreciate your gesture and, believe me, there's nothing I'd like more than for you to wear my collar again."

"But?" asked Frankie, hearing the unspoken word clearly.

"But, we need to talk about the baby and our marriage first," he said gently. He stopped then turned to face her, taking her chin in his hand as he then growled, "Then I'm going to punish you severely for not being honest with me about your feelings."

Despite everything, a little thrill ran through her in response to his words. But she hadn't forgotten the facts. "Does that mean I get to punish you for the same crime?" she asked, lifting her eyebrows questioningly at him.

He released her chin and grinned. "Touché, you got me there. All right, how about we call it quits then?"

"Only if you'll punish me anyway," she retorted cheekily.

He laughed, that gorgeous sexy sound that she loved so much, and took her hand again. They continued walking and soon came across a gravel path that they followed until it stopped by a large stone fountain. The sound of the water cascading downwards was soothing and Frankie was glad when Jake led her to an old wooden bench nearby, where they sat down.

At first neither of them spoke. Frankie stared at the fountain, becoming mesmerized by the comforting combination of movement and sound. Each drop that sprang proudly into the air shattered as it fell onto the water's surface with a loud splash. Her life had been like one of those drops a few moments ago but now a glimmer of hope trickled through her as the lone drop joined the rest of the water and became one again.

"I'm sorry I wasn't more of a support to you after the miscarriage," said Jake, breaking into her thoughts. "I believed you when you said you wanted to be left alone to deal with things your own way. I wanted to give you the time and space to do that. I should have been more insistent that we talk about it but, to be honest, I was actually a bit relieved because it meant I didn't have to face up to my own feelings."

Frankie raised her eyes to meet Jake's and was shocked to see the raw pain in them. How could she not have seen it before?

"When your business took off I was pleased for you because I thought it was helping you to cope with it all," he continued. "I never dreamt that you were using it to cover your grief. I thought you were okay," he added quietly.

"I'm sorry for what I said last night. I didn't mean it." Frankie's face fell as she filled with remorse. How could she have said such a horrible thing?

"I know, sweetheart," he replied. "I can understand why you thought that, to be honest. I'd closed myself off in much the same way you had."

Frankie ran her hand through her hair as she remembered those dark days. She'd turned her back on him to deal with her own pain, but in doing so she'd neglected to consider his. "Is that why you wrote your book?"

He nodded thoughtfully. "Yeah, while I was writing it, I'd lose myself in the story and forget everything else. It became my sanctuary, a place where I could escape from everything."

"Including me," she added. She had a sudden flashback of her cold dismissal every time he'd tried to reach out to her. Shame burned inside her as she recalled her irritation at being disturbed when he'd tried to ask her out to dinner or even offered to make her a cup of tea.

"No, not you, but from the fear of losing you."

Jake looked so sad that her heart contracted painfully in regret. "I didn't realize what you were going through," she said, pushing back a sob. "I resented you for doing so well with your book because I thought you were carrying on with your life as if nothing had happened, but it never occurred to me that you were only doing exactly the same as I was. I'm so sorry."

He pulled her into his arms and squeezed her tightly. "I'm sorry too, sweetheart. I thought I'd lost you," he murmured. "Bringing you here was a desperate attempt to try to salvage our marriage, but I had no idea how you'd react. I thought at one point that you might actually kill me."

"I'm glad you did what you did. It not only made me come to terms with what had happened, but it reminded me of just how much I love you and don't want to lose you." It felt strange speaking so candidly, but also very refreshing.

"So I'm forgiven then?" he asked with a smile.

"Of course—as long as I am too." She hesitated a moment as she tried to phrase the question she should have asked him a long time ago. "How do you feel now? You know, about the baby?"

Jake seemed to give careful consideration to her question, as he rubbed the stubble on his chin. "Until today, I felt like a part of me had died too. I know this sounds clichéd, but it felt as though I'd been living under a dark cloud that, instead of lifting with time, grew heavier and blacker. I needed that outburst this morning," he said with a hint of a smile in his voice, "and Marco knew that too."

"I'm glad you both came out of that reasonably unscathed," said Frankie with a shiver. The thought of what could have happened was too scary to contemplate.

Jake laughed. "Marco could have beaten me to a pulp if he'd wanted to, but he let me batter him with my pent-up emotions and then he watched me cry afterwards. That was what I needed, Frankie, and that's what you needed too. I do understand why you broke down last night and even why you kissed Marco. What's important now is that you feel better for it."

Frankie thought about what Jake was saying. Yes, she had been in desperate need to vent her feelings. It was as if she'd been a bottle of fizzy lemonade that had been shaken to the point where the lid could no longer contain the mounting eruption. Last night the lid had finally blown away and her devastation had been released in a blast that had shaken her to the core. And now? Although she still mourned for her baby, the pain was no longer so unbearable that she had to suppress it beneath a tough façade. Somewhere in her heart there was a new feeling emerging — peace. And regret. Regret that she'd pushed Jake away and treated him so badly.

"I'm sorry for being such a bitch," she said, still not quite able to believe she'd frozen out the man she loved so much.

Jake laughed. "Hey, you were never a bitch," he said, pushing her hair away from her face again. "A scary, bad tempered vixen maybe, but never a bitch."

"Scary, huh? Maybe I should become a switch?" She giggled, knowing full well she'd never want to see Jake on his knees.

"Don't even think it," he growled back, grabbing a handful of her hair and tugging gently. "The only Dom in this marriage is me."

"So does that mean you still want me as your submissive?" Frankie asked, hopefully.

Jake groaned. "Oh, sweetheart, I want that more than you can imagine, but we had to have this chat before we could discuss that. It's important that we've sorted all our other crap out before we can even think about resuming the kink. Do you see that?"

She nodded. "Yes. So, have we sorted through all our *crap*?" She couldn't help smiling at Jake's choice of language. For a writer, he sure as hell had a weird way with words.

"It'll take some time but I think we're getting there, don't you?"

She nodded and smiled.

"There is something I need to know, though," he said, his voice becoming serious again. "Do you blame yourself or the kink for what happened?"

Frankie drew in a sharp breath. Her first thought was to laugh and say that of course she didn't, but that wouldn't strictly be true. She thought carefully before she spoke. "Initially maybe I did," she said, "but I know differently now. At first I was looking for something or someone to blame and it was easier to just blame myself. But, I couldn't cope with that so I turned the blame to the kink and I guess I learnt to live with that belief."

"Is that why you didn't want to continue with our D/s relationship?" he asked.

"Partly, yes. But I was also worried that if I was submissive at home I'd lose the protective barrier I'd built up at work. I know now that that was stupid, but at the time it was how I felt. I think a part of me worried that if I appeared weak, then people would be able to see the broken person I'd become. So I decided to just hide my feelings and act tough."

"I should have seen through your act and helped you," said Jake, regrettably.

"No, I would probably have pushed you away and that might have made things even worse between us. But, despite what I've just said about blame, I want you to know that I don't feel that way now. Everything seems clearer now somehow. I know that what happened was a terrible, tragic accident that couldn't have been helped."

"Remember the doctor said that there's no reason why you can't carry a baby to full term in the future. What I'm saying is, when you're ready we can try again."

Frankie's eyes welled up again and she squeezed Jake's hand hard as she whispered, "When we're *both* ready. But first I want—no, *need* you to be my Master again. I've missed our special dynamic so much, despite my actions to the contrary." She grinned when she saw a glint form in Jake's eyes. *Ooh yes, the Dom is lurking very close to the surface.*

Jake's eyes narrowed as he fixed his gaze sternly on her. Her tummy somersaulted in response and her heart hammered loudly in her chest. He still had such a powerful effect on her. He released her hand and pushed her shoulder down at the same time as glancing briefly at the ground by his feet. She recognized the silent order immediately and quickly slid off the bench to her knees. Keeping her eyes lowered, she sighed with happiness when Jake pushed her head gently onto his lap.

"Thank you, Sir," she murmured in contentedness and almost purred when he ran his fingers through her hair. She'd missed this special connection between them, the mutual understanding that satisfied both their needs in the most exquisite way.

"If I were to get you a permanent day collar, would you wear it?" he asked, softly. "Twenty-four-seven?"

At that moment a feeling of overwhelming happiness bubbled up inside Frankie that she'd never thought possible again. Only a couple of hours ago her whole life had looked broken and shattered and yet here she was, on her knees by her Master's feet. He loved her and he wanted her. And her submission. *Twenty-four-seven. Wow!* They both still had a lot of healing and making up to do, but they'd do it together, sharing their thoughts, both good and bad. One day, she was sure they'd be ready to try again for the family they wanted so badly, but in the meantime, she was more than happy to be Jake's wife, his soul mate and his twenty-four-seven submissive.

"Well?" Jake's voice reminded her that he was still waiting for her answer.

"Oh, yes, Master," she replied happily. "I'd like that more than anything in the world."

Chapter Nineteen

One month later…

"Cheers! Here's to Dominion."

Jake held his glass up and joined in the toast. As he clinked his glass softly with Frankie's their eyes met and his stomach gave a little lurch.

After their chat by the fountain that morning they'd spent the rest of the day alone. They had walked to the village, had a light lunch in the little coffee shop and talked for hours. She'd shared her deepest and darkest thoughts with him and had, in turn, listened when he'd spoken his. On the walk back through the woods, she'd cried and he'd held her tightly in his arms, reinforcing the growing bond that was quickly re-establishing itself between them.

They'd talked about the loss of their baby and had agreed that when they could mention it without too much pain, they would discuss the possibility of trying again. In the meantime, they were going to focus on their marriage and, to his delight, resume the D/s side of their relationship, twenty-four-seven.

When they'd returned from their long walk, Marco had arranged for two female masseurs to pamper Frankie and Christina. Whilst the girls had been enjoying their treatments, Marco had taken him down to the dungeon and given him a demonstration of the single tail whip using a pillow as a guinea pig. It was during this time they had come up with a cunning plan.

When Frankie had returned to their room from her massage, he'd pulled her into his arms and kissed her. Then he'd told her that Marco had invited them to a stay over one night the following month. As it would be a Thursday, the corporate part of the hotel would be open, but as that was completely separate from the East Wing, they wouldn't be disturbed. Marco always kept a few suites free for private guests. It would mean Frankie taking Friday off, though, and Jake was fully prepared to have to work extremely hard to get her to agree.

But, as he had waited for Frankie to object on the grounds of needing to return to work, he'd been astounded when she'd said that she'd love to stay another night.

"But what about your business?" he'd asked in astonishment. Only the day before she'd been desperate to get back to it.

Frankie had just shrugged. "I think Jess can manage things without me for a day or so." Her eyes had sparkled with humor as she'd seen the look of disbelief that must have been written all over his face.

And now, a month later, they were back at Dominion with their friends, sitting around the hearth in the bar. Cleo and Christina were huddled together on a sofa nearby looking like they were in deep conversation. He and Marco both sat in the large leather armchairs opposite the roaring fire while Frankie sat on a furry rug by his feet. Her arms were wrapped lovingly around his legs, a gesture so natural that she probably wasn't even aware she was doing it.

He hadn't actually ordered her to sit on the floor. She'd politely declined the chair Marco had offered her and had instead waited for permission to kneel by Jake's feet. Her smile had lit up her whole face as he'd nodded his agreement and she had almost purred like a kitten when he'd then gently stroked her head as she'd settled.

And now they'd just finished eating the fish and chips that Marco had collected from the village.

"By the way," said Marco, as if suddenly remembering something. "David and his wife, Sinead, asked me to pass on their phone number to you. They'd like to come back for one of the regular club nights and I think they were hoping for some friendly company."

Jake smiled and nodded his thanks. He liked them and was glad they wanted to continue with their newfound kink. From what he'd seen of them on the last night, they'd certainly embraced their roles as Dom and sub—they were naturals. Who knew, one day they might even all share a scene here at Dominion.

The sound of Christina's giggle made them all look across at the sofa. Cleo was whispering something in her ear that was clearly having a strong effect on the younger girl.

"So, what's the story with Christina, then?" he asked, as Marco refilled his champagne glass.

Marco grinned and rolled his eyes. "The little minx has made quite an impression on both Cleo and I. The three of us were up playing until the early hours of that last morning of Vanilla Spice. We finally released her from our clutches as dawn broke," he said with a chuckle.

"Ah, that explains why I bumped into her so early," exclaimed Frankie.

"We've agreed that she can stay on as a trainee house slave," continued Marco, smiling broadly. "We've never had a trainee before so that should be interesting. She's officially starting next weekend although she's barely left since you were last here."

"Good luck with that," said Jake, good-naturedly. "I've got a feeling she's going to be a handful."

"Yeah." Marco chuckled as he clearly relished the challenge of bringing Christina to heel.

Cleo, as if sensing they were talking about her and Christina, stood up and pulled gently on Christina's collar. "I think I'm going to take my little pet upstairs for a while. See you later."

With that she marched Christina across the room. As they passed them, Jake noticed the young girl wink at Frankie and he laughed when Cleo swatted Christina's bottom to make her hurry.

"So what have you two got planned tonight?" asked Marco innocently, leaning back in his chair and crossing his legs.

Jake grinned back at his friend. "Well, I was hoping we could borrow your dungeon."

"Feel free, my friend. Take as long as you want."

"And we'd like you to join us so Frankie can apologize properly for her inappropriate behavior the last time we were here." He patted Frankie's head, aware that she'd be beginning to cotton on to what he was implying.

Since their last visit, they'd spoken about their friendship with Marco and had both agreed that nothing had changed. Jake didn't see him as a threat and knew that Frankie didn't harbor any romantic thoughts about him. Apart from dirty, kinky thoughts, of course.

Marco smiled and nodded. "I'd be delighted." He finished his champagne then stood up and stretched. "I'll just lock up so I'll see you down there."

When they were alone Jake looked down at Frankie. Her face glowed with happiness in the reflection of the fire and her eyes burned with desire. Tonight he and Marco were going to meet every one of her submissive needs. They'd have her screaming in both exquisite pain and pleasure, leaving her begging for more. They would exert their control over her, use her and abuse her in the nicest possible way. They were also going to give her more orgasms than even she could handle.

Oh yes, together, they were going to leave Frankie in no doubt as to her submissiveness. And, just to be sure, last week he'd bought her the most beautiful silver slave collar. When they arrived home tomorrow he was going to place the collar around her neck, with her naked on the floor before him and he'd claim her as his beautiful, precious slave girl.

* * * *

"How many times do you think you earned yourself a punishment the last time we were here, Frankie?"

Jake's question brought a rush of heat to Frankie's pussy and she shifted slightly to accommodate the sexy sensation.

"Er... I don't know, Master," she stammered, not entirely sure where this was heading.

"What do you think, Marco?" asked Jake, gravely.

Marco strode over to the middle of the dungeon floor where she was kneeling, naked, with her arms behind her back. He appeared to think hard, then said, "I think a nice round fifty should do it."

Fifty? Fifty what? As if she didn't know.

"And then there's the little matter of your attitude toward your Master," added Jake. "Hmm, then there's your lack of communication and as for your ability to control your orgasms... How many strokes do you think you deserve, Frankie?"

Well, she knew Marco had already set the figure at fifty so maybe another ten? "Sixty, Master?" she asked cheekily, knowing full well she wouldn't get away with that.

Both Jake and Marco laughed.

"Wrong. Try again." Jake crossed his arms, looking down at her with an air of authority that melted her insides.

"Seventy?" she whispered. *Shit, this is getting serious.*

"Let's round it off and call it a nice even eighty, shall we?"

Crap! "Yes, Master. If you say so."

"Yes, I do." Jake took her arm and pulled her up to stand.

Then Marco knelt in front of her and fastened leather cuffs that were attached to a wide spreader bar, around her ankles. Marco looked up and grinned as her face flared. She knew he'd have a perfect view of her spread pussy. He'd probably also be noticing that she was becoming very wet.

As Marco secured her ankles, Jake bound her hands in front of her with strong rope. Then he pulled them up over her head and threw the rope over a hook in the ceiling before tying it firmly so that she was pulled taught. Marco then started plaiting her hair, interweaving it with more rope. He secured the plait to the length of hemp holding her up so that she was effectively bound by her hair as well as her arms. It was tight, but not painful and it made her feel utterly helpless. She couldn't close her legs, move her body or even turn her head. A rush of moisture seeped out from her pussy and tickled the inside of her thigh as she became more and more turned on.

"Use your safe word if it gets too much, but I somehow don't think you'll want to," said Jake, his breath brushing against her ear.

She shivered. "Yes, Master."

"We're going to take it in turns to flog you, Frankie," drawled Jake, taking her right nipple and pinching it until she gasped from the sexy pain. "Ten strokes each time. You count. At the end of each set of ten we're going to do a little work on your orgasm control. You're such a little hussy that you just can't control yourself, can you, Frankie?"

"No, Master," she whispered, struck, as always, by the powerful paradox of finding such a humiliating admission so erotic.

"Marco, as our generous host, would you like to inflict the first ten?" asked Jake, smoothly. Jake stressed the word 'inflict' and Frankie's tummy somersaulted.

"I'd be honored," growled Marco and strode around Frankie to stand behind her.

"Remember to count or we start from the beginning," reminded Jake, standing directly in front of her.

"Yes, Master."

Marco's hand lightly caressed first one butt cheek then the other. It was incredible how such large, strong fingers had such a feathery touch. *Mmm, that's lovely.*

Then his hand fell heavily onto her buttocks and she let out an involuntary gasp. Fuck, she'd forgotten how hard that man could smack. It felt nice though. She could almost feel the shape of his hand imprinted on her bottom.

"You didn't count, Frankie," growled Marco. "We start again."

Mmm, yes please. "Yes, Sir," she said, trying not to sound too pleased about it.

He smacked her again just as hard and in the exactly the same place. The loud slap bounced off the stone walls and echoed around the airy room. This time it stung a little more, but it still felt good.

"One," she counted out loud.

Then two hard smacks came down in quick succession sending little currents of electricity from the impact point to her pussy. She waited for number four to land just as heavily, but, instead, Marco resumed the soft stroking, his fingers fluttering lightly over her warming flesh. She groaned.

"Ow!" she squealed as number four took her by surprise, harder and louder than before. She barely had time to absorb the sting when the next one fell and Frankie sighed happily as she relaxed into the spanking.

By the time she'd counted ten searing smacks, her bottom was burning and her pussy throbbing. Marco stopped and studied her closely for a second, then reached between her legs and pushed a finger past her delicate folds. She groaned as he circled his finger inside her then she groaned again when he pulled it out and left her empty and needy.

Resigning herself to the fact that that was all she was going to get for now, she waited for Jake to begin the next set of ten. She knew he was behind her so she braced herself for the first smack or rather, the eleventh. Instead, though, she heard a familiar buzzing sound followed immediately by the smooth, cool feel of the wand vibrator. *Oh yeah.* She'd forgotten about the orgasm control.

Even though the wand was set quite low, the insistent buzzing quickly woke the nerve endings in her clit and it wasn't long before the whole area started tingling. *Oh fuck, that feels so good.*

Jake turned up the power and held the head of the wand directly over her clit until she felt the first shudders start to build. This was undoubtedly her favorite toy. Its powerful vibrations reached far deeper, where mere normal vibrators failed to reach.

"Please, Master, may I come?" she gasped as a climax quickly began to loom.

"No!"

"Oh fuck," she cried as her body convulsed with a powerful orgasm that took away the strength in her legs for a moment.

"Oh, dear, Jake, your sub came without permission." Marco laughed as Jake switched off the wand.

Damn, she never had been able to resist that thing.

"I'm sorry, Master," she gasped, knowing full well that Marco had done it deliberately.

"It's my turn to spank you now, Frankie," said Jake, with a devilish edge to his voice. "And I'm going to have to spank you extra hard for being such a disobedient little sub. Start counting from eleven."

"Yes, Master." Despite the fact that she'd been forced to come like that without permission, she was thoroughly enjoying her extended punishment.

Getting spanked and flogged by two gorgeous Doms wasn't exactly a hardship and if they chose to force a few orgasms from her, then who was she to complain?

When Jake gave her three very hard smacks in quick succession he caught her completely off guard. *Fuck, that bloody hurt.* But even as she thought it, the fiery pain started working its magic and soon morphed into the delicious sensations she loved so much.

"You forgot to count again, you naughty girl," scolded Jake. "We start again."

For one awful minute Frankie thought he meant starting from number one again. Sure she loved being spanked, but even she wasn't sure how often she could endure having to start from scratch every time her concentration lapsed.

"I'm sorry, Master," she whimpered.

"We'll start from eleven again."

Thank God.

Yet again he took her by surprise when he only tapped her bottom lightly, barely enough to even hurt. *Harder!*

"Eleven," she growled through gritted teeth, needing more pain.

Number twelve was a ruthless slap right on the backs of her thighs and that one did hurt. A lot. And so the rhythm was set. Where Marco's spanking had been very sensual, Jake's was more brutal, but she enjoyed it just as much. By the time she'd counted to nineteen and braced for the twentieth, her arse was on fire. She could feel the heat reflect off Jake's hand as he stroked it over her reddened skin and knew number twenty would be even harder than the others. And it was. She groaned as his hand scorched the back of her thigh. She'd been expecting him to hit her bottom again so was completely taken aback by his change of target.

"Twenty," she gasped as her body absorbed the fiery pain.

"Good girl," soothed Jake and strode around to stand in front of her. He kissed her hard on the lips then stepped back to be replaced by Marco.

Remaining silent, Marco let go of her chin then reached down and stroked her pussy pinching the delicate skin lightly before moving down to the throbbing heat between her legs. Because they were being forced open by the spreader bar, there was nothing she could do about the moisture trickling slowly out of her pussy. Marco grinned as he ran a finger through the wetness, then brought his hand up and held it in front of her.

"Enjoying this?" he asked in a husky voice.

"Yes, Sir," she whispered, a little surprised that her vocal chords still worked.

"Good."

He brought the finger to her lips and she parted them without hesitation, knowing instinctively what he wanted. He rubbed her juices over them then pushed his finger into her mouth, which she dutifully licked clean. The whole time she didn't take her eyes off him nor did he stop looking into hers. She felt an overpowering urge to kneel before him and succumb to his dominance. Her Master wanted her to submit to this man and that was good enough for her. What her Master wanted, her Master got. She was more than happy to oblige.

Marco must have seen the surrender in her eyes because he grunted his approval then pulled his finger out of her mouth and reached back down between her legs. This time he thrust it inside her hot pussy and she was shocked at how easily it slid in. Blimey, she was soaked. She was also still feeling very sensitive after her guilty orgasm.

She groaned when Marco added a second finger and started finger-fucking her. He wasn't gentle, thrusting deep and fast, just the way she liked it. Because she was still so tender from her earlier climax it didn't take long to reawaken the pleasure points inside her and she whimpered as her internal muscles clamped onto Marco's fingers. She tried moving her body to match Marco's rhythm, but she remained helplessly immobile by the rope and her need increased. Suddenly, completely out of nowhere, a massive wave washed over her and she came again before she could even think about asking for permission.

Marco laughed as he removed his fingers from her bucking body. She arched herself forwards, not wanting to lose his powerful touch and he slapped her pussy in reprisal. Unfortunately this only made her come again and her legs actually gave way as she lost control of them. She swung for a moment, the rope around her hair pulling unbearably tight, until she found her feet again. Through the blur of bliss, she briefly wondered if Marco had known about her weakness for having her pussy slapped.

"Naughty, naughty girl." Jake was laughing as he patted Marco on the back. "Do you see what a little tart I have here, Marco?"

"Hmm, she certainly needs a lot of training. You might want to consider getting a cage," he said with a cruel smile in her direction.

Although the idea of being locked in a cage terrified her, her body told her differently as a wave of heat shimmied through it in response.

"Well, well," drawled Jake, "I do believe she likes that idea."

Frankie closed her eyes as she tried to deny the arousal building inside her at being spoken about as if she weren't in the room. It was humiliating and damned fucking sexy.

"Open your eyes, Frankie," demanded Jake. "I want to see the shame in them as we discuss your disobedience."

She obeyed and, as her eyes opened again, she was stunned when she looked into the faces of two of the most fearful Doms she'd ever seen. Their eyes were alive with raw, primal power and her body shuddered in response. A surge of submissive lust engulfed her as her desire to bow to their dominance filled her with a need so intense it almost hurt.

Both men moved forward until they were either side of her. They were so close she could feel their breath on her ears. Jake's on her right and Marco's on her left. Jake nibbled on the sensitive lobe then whispered, "I love you."

Her heart nearly burst as she turned to him so he could see his feelings reciprocated in her eyes.

"Get ready for the next ten," growled Marco, forcing a shiver to escape from her overheating body.

"Are you ready for more punishment, Frankie?" asked Jake and nipped her earlobe with his teeth.

"Yes, Sir," she whimpered.

"Good, because you've got another sixty to go before you thank us both," he said in a low voice.

Another sixty to go? She closed her eyes and smiled inwardly as she braced herself for the next ten. If what she'd received so far was anything to go by, this was going to get seriously intense. *Bring it on.*

Chapter Twenty

Marco was next to administer the ten strokes. There was no discussion between them as to who was going to do what, when. *Hmm, they must have planned this.* A little thrill charged through her at the thought of them plotting their scene. It made her feel special.

The first stroke kissed the top of her right butt cheek. *Mmm, a heavy suede flogger. Nice.* "Twenty-one," she said quickly before she needed reminding again.

After eight hard strikes in quick succession, Marco gently rubbed her heated skin before delivering two even harder strokes.

"Thirty," she gasped as the last one hit across the tops of her thighs.

They were building up the pressure now, increasing the force of impact as her body adjusted to the onslaught. They were both experienced Doms and knew exactly how hard to hit her at exactly the right time. Unlike her punishment last month, this was purely sensual, designed to build her up slowly so she could take more pain and thereby fly high when she reached the point of no return.

As Marco moved away and put the flogger down, she guessed what was coming next. Sure enough, Jake approached her holding a bullet vibrator in his hand.

"Oh no," she groaned. She was too sensitive for any more stimulation down there. The spreader bar kept her legs ruthlessly spread, and she was powerless to stop Jake as he expertly inserted the vibrator into her pussy and switched it on.

It didn't take long for the pulsing vibes to reawaken her exhausted body. "Ohhhh..." Despite her reluctance, her body responded and her pussy spasmed around the alien object that had been shoved inside her. She was just about managing to hold on when Jake started rubbing her clit. It was so tender that she groaned in discomfort and tried to move away. "No, please..."

He stroked and pinched her clit with the fingers of one hand while he held the vibrator firmly inside her with the other. She couldn't move, couldn't push him away and, despite her reluctance to come again, she couldn't stop the shudders tearing through her body as another climax began to build.

"Please, Master," she groaned.

"What?" growled Jake. "Tell me what you want,"

"Please may I... Argh..." She screamed as her body betrayed her yet again and she lost herself in another intense and powerful orgasm.

As the tremors eased, her body sagged in its bondage, with only the rope around her wrists and hair keeping her up. Jake had bound her wrists in such a way that the rope didn't cut into her skin so she was free to enjoy the feeling of being strung so helplessly up. She was at the mercy of the two Doms and the experience was beginning to go to her head.

She'd only had half a glass of champagne earlier and yet she was beginning to feel a little tipsy.

She became aware that someone was talking to her. *Jake.*

"Frankie, are you okay?"

She smiled drunkenly and nodded. "Yes, Master. Thank you."

Jake smiled and kissed her on the lips. "Good girl. Are you all right to continue?"

"Mmm, yes please," she murmured. She wanted more flogging, more pain, although she wasn't so sure she wanted any more orgasms. She wanted to close her legs, protect her over sensitized clitoris from any more stimulation. But, at the same time, the knowledge that she couldn't do anything to stop them forcing more climaxes from her aroused her all over again.

As she suspected, Jake took over the next set of ten, this time using a lighter leather flogger that had more of a sting in its tail. Where Marco had focused solely on her arse and the backs of her thighs, Jake kept her guessing by whipping her upper back in between the blows to her rear end. The pain was becoming sublime and she was aware that she was teetering on the edge of subspace. She didn't get to experience that very often, so now she welcomed the feeling and hoped the men would take her higher and further into the other world where reality became fused with fantasy.

"How many was that?" Jake's deep voice cut into her euphoric haze.

"Forty," she cried, although that was only a guess. It could have been thirty-eight or forty-five for all she knew or cared.

"Good girl." Jake dropped the flogger and took her nipples between his fingers. He squeezed hard and tugged, pulling her body forwards. The pain was divine and Frankie closed her eyes and smiled her appreciation. *Mmm, more.*

Suddenly something cold and smooth pressed against her bare pussy and a fraction of a second later, an insistent buzzing made her jump in shock. Her eyes flew open as she squealed in discomfort.

"Nooo, please, no," she begged as Marco held the vibrating wand against her aching clit. She jumped in an attempt to close her legs, but the spreader bar did its job and all she achieved was having her hair pulled by the rope.

"Ohhh…" *Fuck, too sensitive.*

"Do you want to come, Frankie?" growled Marco, pressing the head of the wand harder against her bare, naked flesh.

"No, Sir. Please, it's too much."

"That's a shame because *I* want you to come. And your Master wants you to come. So, guess what? You *will* come."

"No, please…" There was no escaping the powerful effects of the wand, which was now becoming seriously painful. Her body shuddered involuntarily as it tried to escape the torment, but there was no respite. Thankfully, before too long the unbearable agony started to build into something pleasurable.

"Oh, oh, ohhhh…" She screamed when her body convulsed violently as another intensely powerful orgasm tore through her. The effect lasted much longer than before and she was powerless to stop herself from jerking violently in the rope. Finally, the waves calmed and she was able to steady herself again.

She was exhausted, her bones felt like jelly and a film of cool sweat covered her skin from the top of her head right down to the tips of her toes. She wasn't sure how much more of this she could endure. It wouldn't be so bad if they just flogged her, but these forced orgasms were killing her.

And so they continued. Marco took care of numbers forty-one to fifty, paddling her hard with a large leather paddle. That was nice. But when Jake knelt between her legs and shoved his tongue into her pussy, the orgasm that he tore from her was excruciating.

Jake then tortured her with a riding crop for numbers fifty-one to sixty. Not only did he hit her across her arse and the backs of her legs, but her breasts got a light beating too. The pain was exquisite and she rode the waves of pleasure each whack brought. But then came the orgasm, forced from her by Marco with the damned wand again.

She swayed in her bonds, intoxicated with the delicious agony being inflicted on her.

"Frankie, are you okay?"

She opened her eyes and met Jake's dark gaze. From the look of pure lust in them, he was enjoying this just as much as she was. Well, maybe 'enjoying' wasn't quite the right word.

He held a bottle of water to her lips. "Here, take a sip of this."

She drank a little then indicated she'd had enough. Jake then nodded at Marco, presumably to let him know to continue with the scene.

Sixty-one to seventy saw Marco produce a long, thin rattan cane. Frankie's eyes widened as he swung it through the air with a loud whistle, and her cry when it hit her bottom echoed through the otherwise silent dungeon. But she was ready for the pain, warmed up so that each searing strike sent her mind soaring through the clouds. She'd lost the ability to count by this time, but the men let her off.

They didn't show any sympathy for the forced orgasms, and when Marco had finished with the cane, Jake shoved a lubricated vibrating butt plug up her arse then finger-fucked her pussy to another screaming climax. As she struggled to recover, Jake removed the butt plug, which only made her pussy spasm again.

Finally, it was time for the last ten. Frankie was vaguely aware of them both striding up to stand in front of her, but it was only when she heard the crack of a whip that her mind snapped back to the present.

"We're going to up the intensity a little bit, Frankie. Can you cope with that?"

Jake's voice reverberated through her head. *Up the intensity? Fuck!* She nodded, her body desperate to feel the kiss of the whip despite her apprehension.

"Answer me, Frankie," insisted Jake. "I need to know that you're aware of what we're going to do and that you're okay with that."

"Yes, Master, I understand and I want it," she managed to say, though her words sounded slightly slurred.

"Good girl. Use your safe word if it's too much."

"Yes, Master."

It was at that point that she realized that Jake was holding a single tail whip. It was his turn to administer the last ten. Was he going to whip her?

Jake must have seen the look of alarm on her face because he kissed her softly on the lips then murmured, "Don't worry, Marco has given me a few pointers and will be on hand to help."

She glanced over at Marco, who she noticed was also holding a whip. *Bloody hell.*

Marco approached her and pulled something out of his pocket. He held his hand up so she could see what he was holding. *Clothes pegs. Oh crap.* He hadn't been joking when he'd said they were going to up the intensity.

Without a word, Marco took her nipple and rolled it between his fingers until it hardened. Then he clamped it with a peg and did the same on her other breast. *Mmm, it hurts but in a good way.*

Then he placed a series of pegs around her breasts and across her tummy. He even put a couple on her bare mound. She swallowed as she absorbed the pain.

Jake walked around to stand behind her while Marco remained in front. Both men stepped away from her, about the length of a single tail whip, to be precise.

"Don't move," growled Marco as he studied her closely.

As if she was going anywhere. She closed her eyes and waited. Her skin tingled in anticipation of the lash and her body shivered with both fear and excitement.

Jake threw the first lash, the tip of the whip landing across her bottom. At first it just felt like a bee sting, but it quickly intensified until it burned through her skin. The level of pain was way higher than any of her previous punishments, but that also meant the level of pleasure was much higher as well.

She groaned as she welcomed the blissful tingling that made her feel as if she were floating on air. *More!*

Then Marco flicked the whip and she screamed. *Ow, ow, ow!* The tip of the whip had actually flicked the peg on her nipple off. The pain was synonymous with that of a nipple clamp being removed but with the added sting of the lash.

Before the agony on her nipple died he did the same thing with the other one, sending the peg flying across the room. Her mind misted up like the windscreen of a car in winter. She couldn't quite see through the fog clouding her eyes and the sound of the whips became muted as reality took on another dimension.

Jake and Marco continued to whip her, Jake focusing on her back and Marco whipping the pegs off her front. She was pretty sure they had reached and passed number eighty, but she didn't care at that point. She wanted them to carry on forever. She never wanted to leave the warm and safe cocoon that encased her aching body. She floated through the atmosphere, smiling at the stars as they winked at her with their sparkly twinkles. Each lash brought her deeper into her sanctuary until she couldn't even feel the sting of the whips anymore.

Mmm. An angel was playing with her hair. *Nice.* Now the angel took her hands and softly massaged them. It's touch was magical, ethereal.

Someone kissed her. *Mmm.* She'd never been kissed by an angel before. Then he whispered in her ear, "Frankie, we're going to let you down now. You're safe, sweetheart, I'll catch you."

Suddenly the pressure on her wrists and hair loosened and her body collapsed into the strong arms of her angel. She smiled drunkenly up into the face of the beautiful entity that was carrying her. He looked a lot like Jake actually. He smiled back and that was the last thing she remembered as she drifted into a gloriously, deep sleep.

* * * *

"Hello, sleepyhead."

Frankie blinked as she slowly opened her eyes. She gazed up into Jake's beautiful face and smiled back as her memory returned. *Wow, so it hadn't been a dream.*

She was huddled in Jake's lap, her legs stretched out along the sofa in the dungeon. He stroked her hair as he looked lovingly down at her with an expression of awe.

"Are you okay?" he asked softly.

"Mmm," she replied. She had tried to speak, but her lips were numb. She tried again. "Yes, Master," she managed this time.

Marco approached the sofa and knelt down in front of her and Jake. He was holding a bottle of water, ice cold judging by the misty condensation coating the outside of it.

"Here, have her drink this," he said and handed the bottle to Jake.

Jake helped her to sit up then unscrewed the cap for her. She took a large swig followed quickly by another. The water tasted heavenly — cold, fresh and very wet. As it ran across her tongue and down her throat memories of the scene flashed before her eyes.

Jake and Marco had clearly gone to a lot of trouble to give her the ride of her life. And it had been. She'd never gone so deeply into subspace before and she had loved every second of her experience. So much so, that she wanted to do it all again.

She marveled at how the two men had worked so closely together to make the scene work. How they'd known exactly what to do and say. They had forced her to come again and again, deliberately denying her the chance to get their permission.

They'd spanked her, flogged her, paddled her, caned her and whipped her, gradually building up the intensity so that she could cope with the pain that had eventually taken her over the edge. Her whole body burned from the punishment it had endured and her pussy was so sore and tender that the mere idea of anything or anyone touching her there made her shiver with horror. And yet she felt more at peace, more satisfied and more loved than she'd ever felt before.

"Thank you, Master," she said to Jake when she'd finished the water. He smiled tenderly and hugged her closer to him.

Then she turned her head toward Marco. "Thank you, Sir."

Marco smiled and gently stroked her cheek. "You're very welcome, petal. I'm going to leave you two alone now. Enjoy the rest of your night. Oh, and come to my private apartment in the morning. I'll cook us all breakfast. Night, night." Marco gave a little salute before disappearing out of the door, leaving Jake and Frankie alone.

"Right, my beautiful little slave," growled Jake, pulling away from her, "now I'm going to fuck you. *Hard*." Flipping her over onto her front he pulled her hands above her head. She giggled and pretended to resist.

He then reached effortlessly down and picked something up from the floor. Handcuffs! Old fashioned metal handcuffs. Real ones with real locks. *Fuck!* Despite her satiated state, excitement tickled its way to her pussy as Jake firmly snapped the cuffs around her wrists. The click of the lock only turned her on even more.

"You may come when you want to," he said, with a hint of dark humor in his voice.

Ha bloody ha. As if she'd be capable of coming after all that erotic torture. Still, her body was ready for him as his weight pressed her down onto the sofa. *Mmm.* He was going to fuck her from behind. She loved that. She tilted her arse upwards slightly so his cock could find her pussy more quickly — she was desperate to be filled with her Master's cock.

"Please, Master, fuck me now," she begged.

Jake chuckled and gathered her hair in his hand. Once he had a firm grip he pulled. *Oh yes!* Then he placed his other hand firmly over her mouth rendering her completely helpless.

"Mmmm," she whimpered as her body gave an involuntary shiver.

Her scream when he drove forcefully into her was absorbed into the large hand clamped over her mouth. With her head held in place by Jake's grip on her hair and his hand gagging her she was powerless to do anything but surrender to her Master's pounding cock.

The harder he fucked her, the harder she needed it. She groaned as his balls slapped against her over-sensitized skin. *Oh fuck, harder!*

How could she possibly be so aroused after having endured so many forced orgasms? But she was and, incredibly, she was on the verge of coming again.

"I hope that butt plug you wore earlier stretched you in readiness for my cock." He removed his hand from her mouth, allowing her gasp to echo around the room.

Jake's words screamed through her head as her need increased. He was going to fuck her arse. Master her, control her, own her. *Oh yes!*

"Please, Master," she begged as he pulled out of her pulsing pussy.

"Please what? Tell me what you want," he growled and reached down for a bottle of lube that had been conveniently placed nearby. With one hand, he expertly squirted the lube over her arsehole. A small amount trickled down and seeped through her labia. She'd forgotten how sensuous the cool lube felt against her burning pussy.

"Please fuck my arse, Master. I need... Oh..."

When Jake's cockhead pressed against her opening, Frankie melted as the ring of muscle just inside her entrance stretched. It had been a while since he'd taken her arse — could she accommodate him? Still holding onto her hair with one hand he reached down and probed her soaked pussy with two rough fingers. He rubbed over her clit with her moisture then pressed his cock a little farther into her arse at the same time.

The old familiar burning discomfort reminded her of how big Jake's cock was, but she knew it wouldn't last long. Once her muscles adapted to his girth, the burn would go away and leave only pleasure. He eased himself in slowly, careful not to hurt her. As he gradually filled her tight channel, hidden nerve endings sprang to life and teased her as the sensations teetered between pleasure and pain.

Finally he was all the way in. *Oh fuck*. She was so full but God it felt good. He pulled back until he was almost out then he plunged back in making her gasp as he took possession of her. Over and over he pulled out then drove back in with a sensuous and methodical motion, until she needed more.

"Harder, Master," she begged.

A deep grunt told her that she was about to get a serious reminder of Jake's possession of her. He plunged back in, this time with a force that almost winded her, then carried on mercilessly pounding her.

He continued to roughly finger her clit until the sensations become so intense that every nerve ending in her body fused together to become one. With each hard thrust into her arse, the pleasure soared. Blood gushed through her veins, her heart hammered in her chest and stars flashed before her eyes as she drew ever closer to the glittering finale. She groaned as everything inside her tightened then screamed as the explosion finally pushed her over the edge. As her body rode the waves of her climax, her heart filled with such love for her Master that it nearly imploded.

When Jake groaned and stiffened inside her, she knew she was about to get her ultimate reward. With one final, deep thrust Jake's cock filled her arse with hot, pulsing cum. Her Master had claimed her.

Jake pulled out then he collapsed on top of her, the sweat on his body mixing with hers, and nuzzled her neck. Neither of them spoke, the moment was too precious for words to express the depth of her feelings and she knew Jake felt the same.

They must both have drifted in and out of a euphoric post-sex doze for quite some time. Eventually though, Jake sat up, freeing Frankie's body from his weight. She shuddered slightly as cool air brushed against her warm, damp skin. He reached above her head and unlocked the handcuffs then gently massaged her reddened skin. *That feels so good.* He stood up and looked down at her with a look of pure adoration and wonder. How could she ever have doubted his love for her? She smiled indulgently up at him and stretched her aching body.

Jake grinned then crossed the room before returning with a thick toweling robe. Draping it over her now shivering body he said, "Come on, beautiful. Let's go back to our room. I'm going to run you a hot bath then, while you're soaking, I'm going to bring us both a nightcap from the bar."

"That'll be nice," she said with a warm smile. "Thank you."

"You deserve to be pampered," he said as he took her hand and led her out of the dungeon. "But remember one thing, Frankie— If you ever keep anything from me again the punishment will be severe."

"Yes, Master," she replied. With a grin, she added, "And if you ever keep anything from me again I'll give you such a hard time you'll have difficulty remembering who the Dom is."

He laughed and smacked her lightly on her tender bottom. "Yes, I've no doubt about that."

As they headed back up the stone steps leading away from the dark cellars, Frankie was amazed at how much things had changed in such a short time.

She was so thankful that Jake loved her enough to have risked everything by delivering his ultimatum. It could have gone horribly wrong—in fact it nearly had. But instead it had been the start of this wonderful new and exciting chapter in their lives. And Dominion would be a part of it. It was a very special place and she was already looking forward to the next time Jake would bring her here and make all her fantasies come true.

About the Author

Katy Swann is in her forties and lives near London, UK with her husband, three children and two cats.

When she isn't writing about strict, sexy Doms putting their strong-willed subs in their place, she likes to read about them. As well as writing, Katy spends her time trying to avoid the housework, keeping the kids from killing each other and drinking copious cups of coffee in the local coffee shop. Coffee and chocolate are the two things that keep her sane and focused, so they're often close by when she sits down to write.

Katy Swann loves to hear from readers. You can find her contact information, website details and author profile page at http://www.totallybound.com.

Totally Bound Publishing